Emma Lee-Potter sp_____
journalist on the Eveni_____
Express and Today. She is now a freelance
writer and editor. She is the author of three
novels for grown-ups, Hard Copy, Moving
On and Taking Sides, all published by Piatkus.
The Rise and Shine Saturday Show is Emma's
first book for children.

the Rise and Shine Saturday Show

Emma Lee-Potter

First published in Great Britain in 2006 by Porthminster Press
www.porthminsterpress.com

A CIP catalogue for this title is
available from the British Library.

ISBN-13: 978-0-9553104-0-9
ISBN-10: 0-9553104-0-7

Typeset in Bembo
by Hope Services (Abingdon) Ltd

Printed and bound in Great Britain
by the CPI Group

For darling Lottie, who inspired the book
And in memory of my fantastic mum Lynda,
who read it and encouraged me every step of the way

Thanks too to Ned, Adam, Charlie, Kit, Mia, my father Jeremy,
my agent Jane Judd, Malcolm Bird, Alan Dart, Sue Lake,
Josa Young and my wonderfully-talented illustrator
Meng-Chia Lai for all their help and advice.

1
Starspotting

ZAZA JONES was numb with cold. Her fingers had turned pinkish-blue and her legs were covered in goosebumps. She'd tried stamping her feet countless times. And blowing hot air on the palms of her hands. But nothing seemed to warm her up.

For the tenth time that morning Zaza cursed the stupid wardrobe department at *The Rise and Shine Saturday Show*. It was a freezing morning in early March and yet instead of kitting her out in thermal undies, fleece and woolly scarf, she looked as though she was off to the beach.

The Rise and Shine Saturday Show had two presenters. Zaza was the scatty blonde one. She wore a purple vest with her name emblazoned across it in white sequins, a tiny pair of pink shorts and lilac flip-flops. Didi Bell, Zaza's bossy older sidekick, had spiky red hair and was wearing her trademark huge silver hooped earrings. She was resplendent in a Union Jack mini skirt, scarlet star-spangled T-shirt and massive red platform heels.

Daniel Drewsome, the show's producer, put his head in his hands when the pair walked on to the set. What were these two like?

'Blooming heck,' he groaned to the floor manager. 'What the blazes do they think they're wearing? Their clothes are supposed to *complement* each other. Just looking at the pair of them is enough to give me a crashing headache. *And* they clash with the sofa. I think I'm going to have to go and lie down.'

1

Zaza and Didi glanced at the famous *Rise and Shine* sofa in horror. They'd taken so long to get ready – Didi had spent a record ninety minutes in hair and make-up – that everyone had forgotten the sofa was an unfortunate shade of pea green with giant yellow spots.

'Oh well,' said Daniel, shrugging his shoulders. 'It's too late to do anything about it now. We're on air in two minutes. You're both miked up, I take it?'

Didi nodded her assent with a gleaming smile. Inwardly, she was livid.

The viewers at home would never have guessed this in a million years, but the stars of *Rise and Shine* couldn't stand the sight of each other. Zaza had never forgiven Didi for spraying her with foam during an item about fire-fighting a few months back. Didi had sworn it was an accident but Zaza knew she was lying. For her part, Didi considered Zaza a complete waste of space.

'She's as much use to *Rise and Shine* as a chocolate teapot,' she repeatedly told the crew backstage.

Every week the girls begged Daniel Drewsome to replace the other. Every week he shook his head and muttered something about their 'dazzling onscreen chemistry.'

'Dazzling' was exactly the right word for them today, thought Daniel as the nine a.m. news bulletin drew to a close and the cheery *Rise and Shine* theme tune burst into the nation's eardrums.

'Anyone got a pair of shades on them?' he asked one of the *Rise and Shine* team. 'Those outfits are making my eyes go all funny.'

Rise and Shine was easily the most popular programme on children's TV. It regularly pulled in five million viewers and Daniel was quietly confident that today's show would attract a bumper audience. Not only did the team have the usual mix of jokes, quizzes and celebrity

2

interviews lined up but most important of all, today Zaza and Didi were going to launch *Rise and Shine*'s long-awaited Starspotter competition. That would really pull the punters in.

The grand announcement was timed for nine-thirty, halfway through the show. First the girls had to wade through an interview with a new boy band called Ladz (one of whom had severe laryngitis and could barely speak, let alone sing). Then came a custard-pie flinging competition (Didi claimed the one that narrowly missed Zaza was just a bad throw) and a live juggling lesson.

Finally the big moment arrived – along with a drum roll and tumultuous fanfare of trumpets.

'*WANNA BE A STAR?*' yelled Zaza, trying to sound as spontaneous and fun as possible. What the viewers didn't know was that both girls read their words straight off the autocue, the sophisticated electronic device that flashed the script up in front of them.

Zaza was determined not to make one of her famous blunders on this one. She still hadn't lived down the embarrassment of one of her false eyelashes dropping off in the middle of last week's programme. Didi had shrieked that Zaza had a big juicy spider crawling down her cheek and plucked it off with a flourish. Zaza had screamed so loudly that it was a miracle none of the camera lenses smashed. Worst of all, she'd completely lost track of what she was saying in the commotion. She'd spluttered and stuttered her way through the rest of the show, vowing to get her own back on Didi next time.

'Yes,' said Didi now, effortlessly following the autocue script. 'If you want to be a pop star, just stick with *Rise and Shine* and we'll tell you how to enter our brand-new Starspotter competition. It's going to be mega …'

Didi turned to Zaza to continue.

'That's right, Didi. Mega. We're looking for talented

3

youngsters between the ages of eleven and fourteen who can sing like, er, er…'

Out of the blue, Zaza was overcome by an attack of nerves. She blinked and struggled to find her place again.

What was she saying?

What on earth was she saying…?

To Zaza's horror, the words on the autocue had turned into one big blur, a blur that didn't make any sense.

'Come on, come on,' urged Daniel from the viewing gallery. 'What are we going to do with that wretched girl? She's driving me up the blinking wall. If she doesn't pull her socks up right now, she's out of here. There are thousands of kids out there desperate for her job.'

'Sing like angels,' said Didi, smoothly taking over Zaza's words. 'You must be able to dance your socks off and have zillions of personality. Our only rule is that you can't be a professional singer or dancer already. You must never have had a record released or performed on TV before and you must have the permission of a parent or guardian. Check on the *Rise and Shine* website for all the details. Now, the most important thing to remember is that we're holding two auditions. Both in the Easter holidays – so you don't have to worry about boring old school. The first is in Manchester on Monday April 7th. The second takes place in London on Thursday April 10th.'

Back on track – and furious that Didi had read *her* part of the script – Zaza immediately retaliated by nicking her co-presenter's next sentence.

'All you have to do is turn up at the following places and the following times,' she said, sneaking a sly look of triumph at Didi. Serve her right for being so mean.

As the venue details flashed onscreen, Didi hissed angrily at Zaza.

'You silly girl. What did you do that for? I was only helping you out.'

4

'No you weren't,' whispered Zaza. 'You were doing your best to make me look like a prize idiot…'

'Well, you don't need any help from me on that score,' murmured Didi. She shot Zaza a withering glance. 'You're doing a pretty good job of it yourself. *And* your bra strap's showing…'

Zaza looked as if she was about to burst into tears but as the camera switched back to the girls once more, she bit her lip and managed to restrain herself. She wasn't going to give Didi the satisfaction of making her cry. Not again.

'Now,' said Didi. 'I know all of you budding pop stars will want to know what's in store for our lucky winners.'

'And that's when things start getting really exciting,' butted in Zaza just a fraction too fast. She was so anxious to stop Didi monopolising the script that she was gabbling her words now.

'*SLOW DOWN*,' yelled Daniel in Zaza's earpiece, making her jump with fright.

'We're not just looking for one star,' she said, slowing to a snail's pace. '*We – are – looking – for – five – stars.*'

Didi glanced at Zaza. What was the matter with the girl? She wasn't Zaza's number one fan, that was for sure, but she didn't usually sound such a blithering imbecile. Why couldn't she speak at a normal speed? She was either jabbering so fast she was incomprehensible or she was drawing out e-v-e-r-y single syllable.

'The judges – and they'll include the top producers, songwriters, dancers and choreographers in the business – are going to choose *five* new stars,' said Didi. 'That's right, I said five. Some from the London auditions. And some from Manchester.'

Didi flashed her perfect white teeth winningly at the nearest camera, waiting for Zaza to take up her next cue.

In fact Zaza was miles away, day-dreaming about what she'd like to do to Didi after the programme. Ram a

5

blooming *Cornetto* in her face, perhaps, or shove her precious Union Jack mini skirt in a bright blue wash. All of a sudden she felt a bony elbow in her ribs.

'It's you,' hissed Didi.

'Er, er, yes,' mumbled Zaza. She searched frantically down the rolling script. Where on earth had they got to? She'd lost her place again.

'From "five,"' prompted Didi again. 'Right in the middle of the screen ...'

Zaza glanced suspiciously at her co-host. She could see the word 'five' on the autocue all right but how could she be sure Didi wasn't trying to land her in it as usual?

Still, it was a risk she was going to have to take.

'That's right,' said Zaza. 'Five. We are looking for five stars. And when we've chosen them we're going to take our five young stars off to a secluded hideaway in the wilds of...'

Zaza tapped her nose conspiratorially.

'In the wilds of ...'

'... A-ha ... now that would be telling,' said Didi. 'But what's important is that our five star winners will get to spend ten days at a mystery location during the summer holidays.'

'They'll be coached by the best people in showbiz,' said Zaza. 'We've got them all lined up.'

'Wicked,' grinned Didi. 'So come on all you budding singers and dancers ... You'd better get practising your tunes and dance routines and we'll look forward to seeing you in Manchester and London. We can't wait, can we, Zaza?'

Looking down on the two girls from the viewing gallery, Daniel's face burst into a rare smile. For the first time in months, Zaza and Didi were working in tandem. Call him a soft-hearted fool, but the pair of them looked as though they quite liked each other.

The producer didn't see what happened once the credits began to roll. Didi wrenched off the tiny microphone hidden down her T-shirt and, confident that no one in the studio could hear her, spluttered: 'By the end of the Starspotter competition, Zaza Fishface Jones, there's going to be one presenter hosting this show and it's certainly not going to be you…'

As the tears streamed softly down Zaza's cheeks, Didi turned on her heel and flounced off the set.

2
Kate

KATE BARNSLEY flung open the front door and wheeled her bike inside the house. Her teeth were chattering with cold and she was wet through but at least she'd finished her paper round for the week. Thank goodness. She could even look forward to a long, lazy lie-in tomorrow. On Sundays the newsagent, Gwenda Graham, delivered all the papers by car.

Today's round hadn't been too bad – apart from the weather and grumpy old Mr Raven at number seventeen hobbling after her shaking his fist and whinging that she'd given him the *Mirror* instead of the *Sun*. 'I'll get you the sack if you get it wrong again,' he'd grumbled at her. 'You see if I don't.'

But otherwise it had been fine. Pedalling through the streets, Kate had kept herself going by warbling snatches of songs inspired by the pouring rain. *'Raindrops Keep Falling On My head,' 'It's Raining Men,'* songs like that. Singing always cheered her up, no matter what. Best of all, she'd finished in record time. It usually took her a couple of hours to deliver the papers on Saturdays. They weren't half heavy, what with all the boring extra supplements and magazines and stuff. But today she was back in time to see the second half of *The Rise and Shine Saturday Show* for a change.

Kate propped her bike against the wall in the narrow passageway. Like all the other houses in the street, the tiny two-up, two-down didn't have a garden – just a minuscule back yard that backed straight on to a grotty-looking alleyway where people came and dumped their rubbish. Then she took off her sodden trainers and tiptoed into the sitting room. Her wet clothes dripped across the carpet, making a funny pattern.

She was anxious not to wake her mum. Saturday was the only day of the week Linda Barnsley could get up late.

Kate wished her mum didn't have to work so hard. She was out at seven-thirty every weekday morning to get to her machining job at Brydale's, the local textile factory. Then on Sundays she was off cooking lunch at the old people's home on the other side of Gribblesdale, the Lancashire mill town where they lived. It hardly paid anything but Linda was too kind-hearted to quit. 'If I hand in my cards, they'd never find anyone else daft enough to do it,' she was forever telling her only daughter.

Kate switched the telly on and curled up on the sofa to watch *Rise and Shine*. She would have liked a cup of steaming-hot tea to warm her up but she didn't want to miss a single second of her favourite show.

Kate grinned at the crazy outfits Zaza and Didi had on. What would she give to wear clothes like that, she thought, glancing down with distaste at her own baggy jeans and holey socks, all sopping wet. It was blatantly obvious that the two presenters weren't seeing eye to eye today. They were so crotchety with each other that it took a few seconds for Kate to grasp what they were on about.

When she realised they were in the middle of launching a new pop competition, she sat bolt upright.

'Manchester – Monday April 7th,' she muttered to herself over and over again, scrambling across the room to find something to write with. In the end she could only find an old copy of the *Evening Telegraph*, stuffed down the side of a chair, and one of her mum's eyebrow pencils.

Linda didn't often wear make-up these days. 'www... oh blast it, what was the website again?'

'What's that, love?'

Kate stared up at her mum. She'd been so intent on trying to scribble the details down that she hadn't noticed her mother appear in the doorway. Linda Barnsley wore a tatty pink nylon nightie with a rip under the arm and a pair of fluffy slippers. One had a pom-pom, the other didn't. Her mousy hair hung limply down her back and she looked completely exhausted – deathly pale, with huge bags under her eyes.

'Oh nothing,' said Kate, trying to hide the paper underneath a cushion. Her mum had enough on her plate without worrying about her. She didn't want to bother her with a pop competition. She'd fret even more.

'Come on, love, tell me. I haven't got the energy to drag it out of you. I'm that shattered I couldn't have the skin off a rice pudding this morning.'

'Really, Mum,' insisted Kate. 'It's nothing. Just a competition I might enter. A bit of nothing. You know me – I'll never get round to it.'

Deep down Kate knew the chances of her getting to the audition were nil. She'd be hard-pressed to do her paper round for a start and even though Manchester was only thirty-five miles away it might as well be the moon as far as she was concerned. She'd only been to Manchester once in her life and that was years ago, when her dad was still around. He'd told her they were going to a posh department store to meet Father Christmas – only when they'd got there he'd changed his mind and taken her to a boring football match instead. And then his team had been thrashed 4-0 so he'd been in a filthy mood all the way back home.

Money was tight in the Barnsley household. That was putting it mildly. Linda Barnsley could hardly make ends meet, and apart from the precious £8.50 a week she earned from her paper round, thirteen-year-old Kate was too young to get a proper job. Even checking the Starspotter details on the *Rise and Shine* website was going to involve a surreptitious trip to the school computer room at break. The Barnsleys didn't have a telephone any more, let alone a computer. The phone had been cut off when Linda Barnsley failed to scrape enough money together for last quarter's bill.

The Barnsleys' life hadn't always been as hard as this. It seemed like another world now but until she was eight, Kate had lived with her mum and dad in a lovely modern house in Primrose Gardens, on the other side of town. It had a proper garden and four bedrooms and a fitted kitchen with a tumble dryer and a microwave. Kate's room had been decorated with bright pink Groovy Chick wallpaper and she'd had her own telly. But then her dad had upped and left them so they'd moved here, to this rented house at 14 Bright Street. They hadn't clapped eyes on him since.

Bright Street, thought Kate, that was a laugh. It should have been called *Grim Street*. Or *Bleak Street*. Bright Street consisted of a long row of redbrick terraced houses on one side and Marshalls, a food processing factory on the other. When the wind was in the wrong direction a horrible smell of rotten eggs wafted across the street. But no one ever complained. It wasn't worth the bother because they knew it wouldn't change anything.

Kate glanced round the sitting room. The red sofa and armchairs had come from their old house, only they were a bit moth-eaten now, and the pink flowery curtains didn't exactly match. Kate wished that the place didn't smell so musty and damp and that the heating worked properly. It had a mind all of its own, the heating. In the summer months, it came on full blast, while now, just

11

when they needed a bit of extra warmth, the radiators were stone cold.

'I'll make us both some breakfast then, love,' said Kate's mum. 'Why don't you switch the telly off and come and talk to me in the kitchen while I do it? I stopped off at Budgens last night and bought some bacon. We can treat ourselves to a good old fry-up. How does that suit you?'

Kate grinned back at her mum. She'd do anything to make things easier for her. Maybe if she won the Starspotter competition and became a mega-famous pop star she'd have the money to buy Linda a massive new house and lots of gorgeous clothes. These days Mum wore her pale blue nylon work overalls most of the time. But you could see that if she didn't look so tired and got all done up for a change she'd still be really pretty.

'Thanks, Mum. That's just what I fancy.'

3
Astoria

TWO HUNDRED miles away in London, Astoria Lennox settled back against a large pile of goose feather pillows and popped a small segment of satsuma into her mouth. She was watching *The Rise and Shine Saturday Show* with mounting fury, utterly convinced that she could do a far better job than that stupid Zaza girl. Zaza was making a right dog's breakfast of everything this morning. For goodness sake, she couldn't even get her words out properly.

Still, thought Astoria, her sulky face brightening a little, she couldn't wait to find out more about the Starspotter competition. She was such a good singer after all – *everyone* said so. She must stand a good chance of winning. The judges would be able to spot talent like hers a mile off.

It wasn't often that Astoria got the chance to watch *Rise and Shine*. She spent most Saturday mornings at Kidstars Stage School in Battersea, where she took singing, dancing, piano and acting lessons. The full Monty, her dad called it.

Pupils had to get to Kidstars at eight on the dot, attired in the stage school's distinctive electric blue uniform – leotards and matching cardigans for the girls and tracksuits for the boys. They had a short break for orange juice and fruit (no horrible E-numbers, everything had to be *super-healthy* at Kidstars) at eleven o'clock and most pupils finished at one. The stage school's critics claimed the regime was far too intense, but the place had produced

13

loads of child stars over the years. One of Astoria's classmates had recently got a small part in *EastEnders* and a boy in the year above had reached number three in the charts a few weeks back with a ballad dedicated to his granny. It was a dead soppy song but Astoria had been green with envy. She would have given anything for it to have been *her* singing live on *Top of the Pops*. He'd even met Girls Aloud.

But Astoria was not the type of girl to be plagued with self-doubt. She knew it was only a matter of time before it would be her turn to catapult into the limelight. Then she'd show them all.

Astoria came from a theatrical family. Her mum and dad, Giselle and Denis – he liked to pronounce it the French way, *De Knee* – were actors. They'd met at the Astoria Theatre, when they were both starring in *West Side Story*. Giselle had been Maria, the heroine, while Denis played Tony, her tough-guy boyfriend from a rival New York gang. Astoria adored listening to her parents' stories about their days in repertory theatre. She never tired of their tales about the different theatres where they'd worked, the stars they knew and the endless succession of parties backstage. Astoria thought it sounded wildly glamorous.

Giselle and Denis Lennox were born romantics. Utterly convinced that their baby daughter was bound to follow them into showbiz, they'd even named her after the theatre where they'd met. When she was little, Astoria had hated her name, wishing that she could be called something less showy, like Isobel or Charlotte. But now she was twelve, she absolutely *loved* it. People always commented on how unusual it was and wanted to know where it came from. And even better, once she explained all about the Astoria Theatre, how her parents had met and fallen in love there, it stuck in their minds.

But today Astoria had a slight sniffle of a cold. The ever-watchful Giselle had insisted she must stay in bed and build up her strength. Astoria didn't argue with her mum. For all her lofty dreams and ambitions, she rather liked the idea of lying in bed all day, watching TV and being waited on hand and foot by her doting parents.

'Would you like a cup of tea and a biscuit, darling?' called Giselle from the kitchen.

'What sort?' yelled Astoria rudely.

'Er, custard creams or digestives.'

'I only like bourbons,' yelled back Astoria.

'That's not what you said last week…'

'Well I've gone off them since then. Bourbons are my favourite now.'

Giselle Lennox had retired from the stage when Astoria was born. The moment she set eyes on her gorgeous blonde, blue-eyed baby daughter she'd vowed to do everything in her power to make her happy. Astoria became the centre of Giselle's universe.

Nothing was too good for her daughter. The Lennoxes weren't well off, but they would far rather go without themselves than deprive Astoria of anything. Now in his mid-forties, Denis made a modest living as a warm-up guy for TV chat show host Bobby Ballard, while Giselle ran an ironing business called Hard Pressed. Astoria frequently complained about the mounds of ironing cluttering up the sitting room of their small ground-floor flat in Streatham, South London. When she was feeling particularly spiteful she slyly knocked piles of immaculately pressed shirts on to the floor, forcing Giselle to iron them all over again. What the spoiled girl didn't appreciate was that if it hadn't been for Hard Pressed, she would have stopped going to Kidstars years ago. Her parents simply couldn't have afforded the stage school's astronomical fees without the money Giselle earned from her ironing. Nor, for that matter, would they have been able to buy Astoria's stage clothes, leotards and dancing shoes. After all, she always demanded – and got – the absolute best of everything.

'Here you are darling,' said Giselle, bustling in with a mug of steaming tea and a plate of custard creams. 'I'm sorry about the biscuits, lovey, I'll pop out and buy some bourbons later…'

'Sssssh Mum,' hissed Astoria rudely as a massive drum roll signalled the launch of the Starspotter competition. She stuffed a custard cream into her spoilt little mouth, showering crumbs all over the bed cover. 'I need to see this bit.'

'What is it, Asti?' said Giselle.

She moved closer to the TV, unintentionally blocking Astoria's view. The Lennoxes only had one telly and Giselle and Denis had readily agreed to Astoria's demands that it should be placed in her room.

'For goodness sake, Mum, *MOVE*, will you? This is really important.'

Knowing better than to get on the wrong side of her daughter, Giselle scuttled out of the room. If it was something important, she was certain Astoria would tell her about it later. She was a good girl really.

4
The Manchester Auditions

Monday April 7th

THE QUEUE for the first Starspotter audition snaked past the Deansgate Theatre, down one side of the street, round the mini roundabout at the end and then back along the other side of the street. Everywhere you looked there were crowds of teenagers laughing and chattering and jumping up and down with excitement. The girls outnumbered the boys by about five to one and while the girls were dressed up to the nines, the boys shuffled about in scruffy old jeans and trainers looking a bit embarrassed.

The auditions were due to start at ten a.m. but lots of the contestants were so keen they'd been queuing all night, like bargain hunters waiting for the January sales. A few ultra-keen wannabes had planned the audition like a military exercise and had arrived equipped with blankets, sleeping bags and enough food to feed an army.

Kate gasped as she rounded the corner and saw the crowds. She couldn't believe she was here. It had taken four weeks of paper rounds to save enough money to afford two return train fares from Gribblesdale to Manchester Piccadilly. And nearly as long to persuade her mum to let her enter the competition.

'It's only because I don't want you to be disappointed,' Linda Barnsley kept telling her.

'At least let me have a go,' pleaded Kate. 'I promise I won't make a fuss if I don't get through. I'll just shut up about it and get on with my schoolwork. I won't ever complain about anything again. Honestly I won't.'

'But they're only running the competition in the first place because it makes good telly. I couldn't bear it if some horrible, nit-picking judge said critical things about you. It would break my heart.'

'Course they won't do that,' said Kate. 'Constructive criticism – that's what they call it. And anyway, I'm tough. I can cope.'

Linda doubted that. But finally she'd given in – on the condition that she came too.

'You're only thirteen. You're far too young to go all that way by yourself.'

Kate bit her lip and kept silent. There was no point in making a fuss and deep down she was glad her mum would be there to hold her hand.

Once they were installed at the end of the queue, a man in a lime and pink *Rise and Shine* T-shirt came and handed Kate a green ticket with the number 516 printed on it.

'What's that?' asked Linda, peering over Kate's shoulder. 'A raffle ticket?'

'Don't think so,' said Kate. 'I think it probably means I'm 516th in the queue.'

'Oh dear,' said Linda. 'We're obviously in for a very long wait.'

She took an old-fashioned tartan flask out of her bag and poured them each a cup of tea. She'd brewed it at the crack of dawn so it wasn't piping hot but Kate gulped it down gratefully all the same. She'd read in a magazine somewhere that it was important to drink lots of fluids.

'How long do you think it'll take?' said Linda. 'Two hours? Three? Sixteen?'

Kate glanced at her watch. It was ten past ten.

'Haven't a clue. I wish they'd hurry up and get us

18

moving. I can feel the butterflies in my tummy.'

'Calm down, love. You're going to be fine. You've got a lovely voice.'

Linda took hold of Kate's hand and rubbed it vigorously.

'Whatever happens, it will be something to tell your grandchildren,' she told Kate.

'You what?' said Kate. She was so pent-up she couldn't concentrate on anything. Robbie Williams could have walked past and she wouldn't even have noticed.

'Oh, nothing.'

Linda turned her attention to the other contestants. Some of them looked *so* grown up. It was hard to believe they were no older than fourteen. Take the girl in front of them. She could easily have walked straight out of *Top of the Pops*. Heavily made-up, she wore skin-tight leather trousers and a tiny crop top that showed off a tanned midriff with a pierced tummy button. Her hair was white blonde and teased into tiny ringlets that cascaded down her back like a waterfall. In contrast, Kate, wearing an old *Sugababes* T-shirt and jeans, with her long dark hair newly-washed and tied back in a simple pony tail, looked like a babe in arms.

At that moment Leather Trouser Girl leaned over and whispered something to the woman standing next to her. She looked as hard as nails, thought Linda. Thank goodness her Kate wasn't like that.

The woman in front of them laughed and put her arm round Leather Trousers.

'I don't see how they'll find out,' she muttered conspiratorially. 'It's not as if they asked you to bring your birth certificate along, is it?'

Linda glanced at Kate. Had the woman just said what she thought she'd said? But Kate was miles away, oblivious to everything.

Linda wrestled with her conscience for a few seconds, then plunged in regardless.

'Excuse me,' she said, tapping the woman on the shoulder.

'You what, love?'

The woman swung round to face Linda. She was immaculate, with cool blue eyes and a sleek blonde bob that looked a bit like a helmet. Her fuchsia-coloured trouser suit and high black patent boots probably cost more than Linda earned in a whole month.

'I'm sorry to butt in but did you say something about needing a birth certificate? I'm just a bit anxious because my daughter hasn't brought ...'

Helmet Hair's eyes narrowed with fury.

'How dare you listen to other people's conversations?' she retorted, glaring at Linda. 'What a cheek. And I didn't say anything whatsoever about birth certificates. Why on earth would you need one here? Are you completely mad? Why don't you mind your own business?'

It was obvious why the Starspotter contestants might need a birth certificate, thought Linda. And that was to prove they were aged between eleven and fourteen – as the competition rules so clearly stated. With a flash of insight, she suddenly understood why Leather Trousers was so jittery. No way was this girl fourteen. Sixteen or seventeen more like.

Anxious to keep the peace, Linda stepped back. There was no point getting embroiled in a heated discussion with this pair.

'Forget it,' she muttered. 'Forget I spoke. I'm just a bit nervous, that's all. It's a bit nerve-wracking all round, isn't it?'

Helmet Hair didn't grace this with a reply. She spun round on her heel and began whispering to her companion once more.

20

Linda wasn't sure whether to be thankful that she'd avoided a row – or furious that another contestant was blatantly flouting the rules. She shrugged her shoulders. What did it matter? She and Kate would be on the train back to Gribblesdale by lunchtime. What could she do to cheer Kate up when they got home? Her face brightened. They'd stop off at the chippy as a treat. That would help ease the disappointment.

At that moment a murmur of excitement rippled through the crowd. A gleaming navy blue limousine with blacked-out windows swept past and drew up in front of the theatre.

'Who's inside?' said Kate, craning her neck to try and get a better view. They were so far down the queue that it was tricky to see anything, but she could just make out two girls in matching purple outfits. They paused to wave to the crowd for a split second, then dashed inside.

'It's Zaza and Didi,' cried Kate, turning to her mum. Her eyes shone with excitement. 'I never dreamed they'd be here. Wow, Mum. I keep having to pinch myself to believe that this is really happening. But it is, isn't it?'

'Yes, love,' said Linda. She squeezed Kate's hand lovingly, touched by how little it took to please her daughter. 'It really is.'

The excitement of Zaza and Didi's arrival soon wore off. By one p.m. Kate and her mum were still waiting, tired, hungry and fed up to the back teeth with queuing. Kate, who'd been up at the crack of dawn as usual to do her paper round, wondered how much longer it would take to reach the front. They'd finished the flask of tea and devoured the *KitKats* Linda had stuffed in her pocket. At one point Linda had gone to buy sandwiches from a hot dog van outside the theatre. But when she saw the extortionate prices she changed her mind. She didn't have enough money for one sandwich, let alone two.

'Sorry, love,' said Linda when she returned to Kate's side. 'They didn't have the sort you like. We'll have to wait till later.'

'Doesn't matter,' said Kate, forcing a smile. She knew her mum was lying but she didn't let on. Poor Mum. She worked so hard. Kate didn't want her to feel any worse than she already did.

It was two forty-five by the time Kate and Linda finally got to the front. Kate was so ravenous that she was worried she might faint if she didn't eat something soon. But as soon as they stepped into the foyer and joined yet another queue to register for the competition, a cheery-looking girl with her hair in crazy bunches appeared holding a tray piled high with sandwiches. She wore pink satin knickerbockers, a matching *Rise and Shine* T-shirt and lime green trainers.

'Complements of the *Sooper Dooper TV Company*,' she said with a flourish. 'Help yourself.'

'It's very kind of you,' said Linda gratefully. She and Kate took a couple of sandwiches each.

'It's the least the company could blooming do,' muttered the sandwich girl under her breath. 'I mean, all these poor boys and girls. Queuing for hours in the cold like that. Between you and me, I think Daniel Drewsome has bitten off more than he can chew this time.'

'Who's Daniel Drewsome?' asked Kate.

'Producer of the show,' said the girl crossly. 'The Starspotter competition was all his bright idea but he didn't have a clue how many people would turn up to the auditions. It said on the lunchtime news there are about a thousand kids here today. I mean, it's fine when you're holding auditions for grown-ups but you can't treat kids like this. The papers will have a field day if they find out that we've let hundreds of kids wait in the street for hours.

Oh blooming Nora, you're not from the press, are you?
I'd better watch what I say.'

'No,' giggled Kate, munching hard on her cheese and
tomato sandwich. 'Mmmm, this is delicious. And anyway,
we don't really mind. It's more exciting than sitting at
home.'

'Go on, have another one,' said the sandwich girl. 'You
look as if you need feeding up a bit.'

'Thanks,' beamed Kate. 'I will.'

Linda had taken an immediate liking to the *Rise and
Shine* girl. No one else from the show had bothered to tell
them anything. A friendly face and a bit of sympathy made
all the difference in the world.

'Do you work on *Rise and Shine*?' she asked the girl.

A cloud of irritation appeared on the girl's face.

'I'm afraid I do.'

'Wow,' said Kate. She couldn't believe she was actually
talking to someone important. 'So you know Zaza and
Didi?'

'I certainly do,' said the girl. She didn't sound very
pleased about it.

'It must be really exciting working with them.'

'Exciting,' repeated the girl thoughtfully. 'Mmmm, it's
exciting all right. What with Didi trying to grab the
limelight for herself all the time and Zaza constantly
throwing wobblies. Yes, you're right. Exciting's definitely
the word for it.'

Kate looked puzzled. If she worked with Zaza and Didi
she'd be the happiest girl in the universe. She wished she
had a job like that. It must be such fun.

Seeing Kate's confusion, the girl felt guilty.

'Oh look. I'm sorry. Don't listen to a word I say. It's
been a long day and we've still got loads of kids to see.
Working on *Rise and Shine* has its moments but it's great.
Just great. I'm Dottie Birch by the way. Who are you?'

23

'Kate,' said Kate shyly. 'Kate Barnsley. And this is my mum. She's called Linda.'

'Lovely to meet you both,' said Dottie, holding out her hand. 'Now Kate and Linda, where are you from?'

'Gribblesdale. In Lancashire.'

'Gribblesdale,' said Dottie. 'Never heard of it. But then geography never was my strong point at school. If I'm honest I'm amazed I managed to get to Manchester at all. I had to drive the *Rise and Shine* van with all the posters and props and stuff. All by myself. I was scared stiff I was going to end up in Cornwall or somewhere. So what's Gribblesdale like when it's at home, anyway? Is it nice?'

Kate and Linda looked at each other and burst out laughing. Nice was *not* the word to describe Gribblesdale. They were quite fond of it – it was home after all – but it wasn't exactly guidebook material. The most famous landmarks in Gribblesdale were the gas works and the food processing factory.

'Yes, it is,' said Kate loyally. 'It's very nice.'

'I'll have to take a trip there, won't I?'

Kate stuffed the last bit of sandwich into her mouth and nodded. She couldn't imagine Dottie driving the *Rise and Shine* van up Gribblesdale High Street in a million years.

'How much longer d'you think we'll have to wait?

Kate was starting to get nervous again. Everyone else looked so trendy and super-confident. One girl was belting out a Kaiser Chiefs number at the top of her voice while loads of people were hopping about practising their dance steps. And how on earth would she ever stand a chance against a glamour-puss like Leather Trousers?

Kate stood on tiptoe to see where Leather Trousers had got to. There was such a scrum that it was difficult to spot her. But finally she clocked her and Helmet Hair standing in the corner with a couple of men wearing *Rise and Shine*

T-shirts like Dottie's. Helmet Hair was gesticulating wildly. She looked absolutely livid.

'Around twenty minutes or so, I should think,' said Dottie.

She peered closely at Kate.

'I say, are you all right? You look dreadfully pale.'

'Just a bit nervous, that's all,' said Kate, trying to sound cheerful.

'Look, don't worry,' said Dottie. 'I'll see if I can have a word with someone. Get you in a bit sooner than that maybe. Can you just hang on here a sec?'

Linda grabbed hold of Kate's hand. It felt icy-cold.

'Don't worry. We're not going anywhere. Are we, love? I don't think we could, even if we wanted. We're a bit wedged in.'

Dottie barged her way out of the foyer, carrying her tray of sandwiches aloft. A minute later she was back, her face wreathed in smiles.

'Sorted,' she yelled at Kate. 'Come on, if you follow me, I'll tell you something really funny.'

Dottie sounded so cheerful that for a moment Kate forgot her terror. She and Linda dutifully followed Dottie up a flight of red-carpeted stairs and across a vast landing.

'What were you going to tell us?' Kate asked Dottie as she hurried to keep up.

'You'll never believe it. The blooming cheek of some of these kids. We've already had a nine-year-old trying to pass himself off as twelve and another lad doing his best to jump the queue by climbing through the window of the ladies' toilets. And now this. Did you see that girl downstairs? You know, the one with dyed platinum hair and leather trousers who really fancies herself?'

'Yes,' said Kate. She knew exactly who Dottie meant.

'Well, guess how old she is?'

25

'Well, she's certainly more than fourteen,' retorted Linda. 'Sixteen or seventeen, more like.'

'Wrong,' chortled Dottie. She plonked her sandwich tray on the carpet and did a little jig of delight.

'What then?' demanded Linda.

'She's only blooming nineteen,' chuckled Dottie. 'She's called Lara Linklater and she's a professional dancer already. One of our production guys recognised her. She was in some musical in the West End a few months back. Got a blooming cheek, hasn't she? Fourteen, my foot.'

Kate giggled. She felt an awful lot better all of a sudden.

'Right Kate,' said Dottie, taking her by the arm. 'Listen to me. Keep that megawatt smile on your face and speak up when Daniel Drewsome asks you anything. He's sitting in the front row and he's in charge. In fact, don't just speak up – *BELLOW*. Yes? Every time you're worried you might dry up just remember our friend Lara trying to make out she's fourteen. She should have come in frilly knickers and ankle socks, shouldn't she?'

Kate burst out laughing at this. She and Linda followed Dottie through a pair of mirrored doors and into the auditorium. Kate gasped at the size of it. The only theatre she'd ever set foot in before was Gribblesdale Memorial Hall, with its rickety stage, wooden seats and dire amateur pantos.

'Wow,' she gulped, glancing at the ornate golden roof and plush red velvet seats. The stage looked about half a mile away. A boy the size of a pin was belting out *Mustang Sally* for all he was worth, watched by about ten shadowy figures in the front row. A posse of cameramen onstage followed the boy's every move.

For a split second, Kate stood as still as a statue, so terrified she was incapable of moving. Then quick as a flash she turned, ready to make a run for it.

Linda was too quick for her. She grabbed hold of Kate's

hand, gripping it with surprising strength for someone so tiny.

'Oh no, you don't,' she whispered under her breath.

'What d'you mean?' said Kate, her voice wobbly with fear. 'You didn't want me to audition in the first place.'

'I know,' said Linda, still holding Kate's hand firmly. 'But now you're here, you've got to give it a go. You'll never forgive yourself if you don't at least try. Come on, sweetheart. You can do it. You know you can.'

'Your mum's right, Kate,' murmured Dottie. She twiddled one of her bunches thoughtfully for a moment. She'd taken a liking to the ultra-modest Kate – the girl was a breath of fresh air compared to some of the prima donnas she'd had to cope with today. 'Look – if you give it your best shot up there, how about me fixing for you to get Zaza and Didi's autographs backstage afterwards? What d'you say?'

Kate's face lit up with gratitude.

'That would be amazing. Could I really?

'Yep, you really can,' said Dottie. She grabbed Kate's other hand and hurried her down towards the stage. Kate was so stunned by the thought of meeting Zaza and Didi that she stumbled along on autopilot. She barely even noticed when Linda took a battered old make-up case out of her bag and dabbed circles of blusher on her face as they walked.

'You need a bit of colour in your cheeks, love.'

When they got to the front, a man wearing a massive pair of headphones fastened a tiny microphone to the top of Kate's T-shirt. Someone else jotted down Kate's details on a clipboard and then a homely-looking woman in a headscarf took a Polaroid picture.

'Give us a smile, lovey,' she said in a friendly sounding voice. 'You look like your dog's died.'

Kate grinned at this, her face lighting up in a wide smile.

27

'I haven't got a dog,' she grinned.

'That's better, lovey. You're a stunner when you do that.'

'Thanks, Rose,' said Dottie, leading Kate up some steep wooden steps and straight onto the stage.

'She's the *Rise and Shine* tea lady,' whispered Dottie.

'Who?'

'Rose. The lady with the camera.'

Mystified as to what Dottie was on about, Kate gazed across the auditorium. She had never seen such a gigantic theatre in her life. It was almost the size of Gribblesdale.

Dottie deposited her in the middle of the stage, beneath a panoply of dazzlingly bright lights, and then ran to the side. Dottie gulped fretfully. She felt as if she had abandoned a tiny puppy. Kate looked so vulnerable standing there by herself.

'*NAME?*' bellowed a voice.

Kate blinked. She assumed this was the dreaded Daniel Drewsome Dottie had been on about, but the stage lights were so intense she couldn't see anything at all. It was like peering into a big black hole.

'*NAME?*' snapped the voice again, more impatiently this time.

'Kate Barnsley.'

'If you can't talk louder than that sweetheart, how d'you think we'll be able to hear you sing?' yelled the voice. 'Let's try one more time or you're off. *NAME*?'

'*JUST SHOUT,*' hissed Dottie from the side of the stage.

The thought that Dottie was rooting for her a few yards away changed everything. It was as if a light flicked on inside Kate's head. In an instant, she put aside her nerves and began to enjoy herself.

'*KATE BARNSLEY,*' roared Kate for all she was worth.

'*AGE AND SONG,*' shouted the voice.

'I'm thirteen,' said Kate, quick as a flash. 'And I'm going to sing *River Deep, Mountain High*.'

Kate had grown up listening to the celebrated Ike and Tina Turner song. It was an all-time favourite in the Barnsley household from way back. Kate could even remember her mum and dad belting it out in the kitchen at their old house when she was four. Her mum had a great voice – easily as good as Tina Turner's.

Perched on the edge of a seat halfway up the stalls, Linda Barnsley felt a lump in her throat as Kate launched into the familiar song. Wow. She was used to Kate singing at home but until that moment she hadn't realised how powerful her daughter's voice was. Not only that. She was amazingly in tune. Even without an orchestra to accompany her, she hit every note bang on.

The people in the front row seemed pretty impressed too, because when Kate got to the end they clapped for ages.

Then, as quickly as it had begun, it was over.

'Thanks Kate,' boomed a male voice. 'Mmmm. Pretty good. You've got a big voice for a small girl, haven't you? Watch the show on Saturday and you'll find out if you're through.'

Kate blinked. She couldn't believe that the moment she'd been dreaming about for weeks was over. Her moment of stardom, standing on the stage of the Deansgate Theatre, had come and gone.

In the midst of the excitement, Kate completely forgot Dottie's promise. She rushed straight into Linda's arms, desperate for a reassuring hug. When she turned to look for Dottie a few seconds later, the *Rise and Shine* girl had vanished into thin air. Kate's heart plummeted with disappointment. She'd so wanted to thank Dottie for her kindness and encouragement. Not to mention the sandwiches. She couldn't have done it without her.

'Come on, love,' murmured Linda softly. 'You were sensational. I was so proud of you singing your heart out up there. But now it's time to go home. Back to real life, I'm afraid. Back to Gribblesdale.'

It wasn't until she was standing on the platform at Manchester Piccadilly, waiting to catch the train back home, that Kate remembered the autographs. She sighed crossly. It would have been good to have something to remember Starspotter by. To show her mates at school. How could something so important have slipped her mind?

Over the next few days Kate forced herself to put the competition out of her mind. Apart from Sally Wilson, her best friend, whom she swore to secrecy, she didn't tell anyone. There was no point. The judges were only going to choose two or three contestants from the Manchester auditions. She didn't stand a chance.

At seven-thirty on Thursday morning the doorbell rang long and hard. Linda had already left for work so it was Kate who opened the front door. A cross-looking postman stood on the step with a stack of post in his arms. Kate glanced bleary-eyed at her watch. She'd overslept. Mrs Graham at the newsagents would be hopping mad.

'Thanks,' said Kate, grabbing the pile of brown envelopes. Oh dear, that would get Mum in a state – Linda was worried enough about bills as it was. Sifting through them, Kate noticed that each one had phrases like 'Council Tax – Urgent' and 'Inland Revenue' stamped across them. All except the last, a large brown envelope that was too big to stuff through the letterbox. On the front, written in the most scrawly handwriting Kate had ever seen, was the name *Ms Kate Barnsley*. Kate chuckled out loud at the writing. Mr Scrafton, her English teacher, would have apoplexy if he saw it. He thought Kate's writing was abysmal – he should see this …

Kate was puzzled. Who on earth could it be from? Kate rarely wrote letters so she couldn't think *who* had written to her. The envelope was postmarked London. That was even more puzzling – Kate didn't know anyone in London.

She tore open the wrapping impatiently. Inside was a shiny purple hardback book with the word *Autographs* stamped in silver lettering. Opening it up, Kate saw that the first page was covered in signatures. The rest of the book was blank.

'To Superstar Kate, Good luck in the competition, lotsluv, Zaza,' said one entry. Written in red felt-tip, it was accompanied by loads of kisses.

'To Kate, Sorry not to meet you. Keep watching the show. Best wishes, Didi,' said another, far less effusive message.

The page had also been signed by other members of the *Rise and Shine* crew. And right at the bottom – written in the same atrocious scrawl as the envelope – was a big smiley face and the following message. *'See? I didn't forget. Loads of love, Dottie.'*

31

5

The London Auditions

Thursday April 10th

A STORIA LENNOX didn't like waiting for anything. She was always the first in her class to wear the latest fashions. She had all the coolest downloads and her ears had been pierced way before anyone else. Well, Naomi Glass, a girl from the year above at Battersea Comprehensive, the school she attended during the week, had got hers done at about the same time. But Astoria had definitely been first at Kidstars.

When Astoria turned up to the London Starspotter auditions, however, she had to wait her turn for a change. Just like everyone else. She clicked her tongue in annoyance – but there was absolutely nothing she could do to jump the queue.

Astoria had arrived at the Strawberry Hill Studio in Kensington flanked by both her parents. Giselle Lennox was staggering under the weight of two huge bags containing everything her daughter might need. The contents ranged from three changes of clothes – true to form, Giselle had been up till late last night ironing them – to a photo album showcasing Astoria's past stage triumphs and an iPod in case she got bored. While Astoria and Giselle stayed put in the queue, Denis Lennox made regular sorties to check how fast it was moving, before dutifully reporting back to his wife and daughter.

The *Rise and Shine* team had learned its lesson from the Manchester auditions, where the hordes of youngsters had grown cold, hungry and fed up with waiting. In London, everything from drinks and snacks to street entertainers had been laid on. A clown on stilts juggled a staggering assortment of hoops at one end of the queue while a fire-eater terrified the living daylights out of the contestants at the other. One girl was so scared by the sight of him plunging a flaming torch down his throat that she had to go home.

Astoria wasn't remotely interested in any of it. Each time someone offered her a chocolate bar or a fizzy drink, she wrinkled her nose with distaste and explained she never let anything so unhealthy pass her lips. This wasn't strictly true, of course. She had conveniently forgotten her fondness for bourbon biscuits, *Fanta Fruit Twist* and salt and vinegar crisps.

'Right snotty one we've got here,' muttered one of the *Rise and Shine* assistants under his breath. Astoria had just asked if he could possibly get her a cup of peppermint tea to calm her nerves.

But Astoria was oblivious to comments like this. She was far too busy planning what she was going to say when the judges raved about her performance. They were bound to recognise talent when they saw it.

'Coo-eee,' shouted a voice in the crowd behind her. 'Astoria. Over here.'

Puzzled as to who was yelling her name, Astoria swung round.

Her face hardened at the sight of Stryker MacKenzie, another Kidstars pupil. What did he think he was doing here? For goodness sake, he was fine doing panto and slapstick but there was no way he could ever be a pop star. Stryker's voice could shatter a window at thirty paces. And he didn't exactly look the part either – with his short ginger hair and big pudgy face. Even on a good day he looked like he'd gone ten rounds with Lennox Lewis.

33

'Hi,' she said in a frosty voice, then turned her back on him and tried to engage her mum in animated conversation. She certainly didn't want the *Rise and Shine* people to think she had anything to do with Stryker MacKenzie.

Astoria was even more livid when she noticed Max Harrison a few yards ahead of her in the queue. Stryker's presence was irritating enough but how did Max have the brass neck to be here? Max was the boy in the year above her at Kidstars who'd got to number three in the charts with a yucky song called *My Granny's Grand*. It was so sickly that most of his year made vomiting noises when he walked past.

Astoria looked as though butter wouldn't melt in her mouth but she scarcely had a single charitable thought in her head about her fellow Kidstars students. She was terrified in case they became stars before she did.

She was thoughtfully biting into a stick of raw carrot (prepared by Giselle at the crack of dawn) when she caught Max Harrison's eye. He grinned merrily at her and waved.

'You've got no chance against me, Storybook,' he yelled at her. 'No chance at all. Your voice is like a foghorn.'

'Is that one of your friends from Kidstars, darling?' Giselle Lennox asked.

Astoria was seething. Not only at Max being here in the first place – but also at the nerve of him calling her Storybook in front of all these people. She loathed the nickname and he knew it.

At that moment a girl in a lime green *Rise and Shine* T-shirt, cerise knickerbockers and plaits walked past bearing a tray of drinks. In a flash Astoria had a brainwave. She knew how to shut Max up good and proper.

'Excuse me,' she called out.

34

'No probs,' said the girl. 'D'you want a drink? Coke? Lemonade? Orange juice?'

'No, no, nothing like that,' shuddered Astoria. 'No, it's just that I seem to remember Zaza and Didi saying something about us not being able to enter if we'd had a record released already. Is that right?'

'Ye-e-e-s,' said the girl slowly. 'Why? Is there a problem? My name's Dottie Birch – I'm the assistant producer cum dogsbody round here. Who are you?'

Astoria glanced down, doing her best to look demure.

'Astoria Lennox. And there isn't a problem. Not really. Well, not as far as I'm concerned, there isn't. But I thought you should know that that boy over there – do you see, the one in the Eminem T-shirt? He goes to the same stage school as me and he's just had a record in the Top Ten. *And* he's been on *Top of the Pops*.'

'Has he now?' said Dottie, her eyes narrowing thoughtfully.

'So it wouldn't be fair if he auditioned for Starspotter, would it?'

'No, it most certainly wouldn't,' said Dottie. 'Don't worry, sweetie. I'll sort him out.'

Astoria watched gleefully as Dottie marched up to Max and began whispering in his ear. She couldn't hear what they were saying but Max's face flushed a deep shade of crimson. Dottie punched a string of numbers into her mobile and within minutes two *Rise and Shine* heavies had hauled the boy out of the queue and sent him packing.

A spiteful grin appeared on Astoria's face. That would teach Max Harrison to call her Storybook.

As well as laying on food and entertainment for everyone, the *Rise and Shine* crew had tightened up their time-keeping in the few days since the Manchester auditions. Instead of having to wait for hours on end to perform, the contestants were divided into two groups the moment they set foot in Strawberry Hill. The girls were despatched into one studio to perform, the boys into another.

When Astoria reached the reception desk, a bored-looking girl with cropped red hair and two gold studs in each ear jotted down her details and directed her to Studio Alpha. Giselle and Denis dutifully trotted behind their daughter, still weighed down by all Astoria's baggage. At the studio door, however, the couple were barred from entering by a heavily-built security guard in a navy blue uniform.

'Sorry,' he said, holding up a giant-sized hand. His knuckles had the letters ELVIS tattooed across them. ''Fraid it's contestants, judges and camera crew only from here.'

'Good luck, darling,' fussed Giselle, smoothing Astoria's blonde hair behind her ears. Astoria promptly flicked it out again.

'Go and knock 'em de ...' Denis's voice trailed away into nothing. Before he could even finish his sentence, Astoria had skipped through the door without a backward glance and was gone.

Studio Alpha was a large square room, with a microphone on a stand at one end and a long, narrow table at the other. There were four windows down one wall, each covered with thick black curtains to shut out the outside world, and dazzling studio lights. Behind the table sat Zaza Jones, together with Dottie and a bored-looking man in a grey suit. This was Dougie Barton, one of the best-known music producers in the business. They all had endless sheets of paper scattered in front of them.

For the last few minutes, in between the departure of an eleven-year-old contestant who'd sung *Long-haired*

Lover From Liverpool completely out of tune and Astoria's arrival, Dottie had been doing her best to cheer Zaza up.

Much to Dottie's amazement, Daniel Drewsome had tapped her on the shoulder half an hour earlier and summoned her to come and help with the judging. Dottie couldn't think why he wanted *her* there. Dougie Barton knew the music business backwards after all. Surely he and Zaza were capable of picking out who could sing and who couldn't? Mind you, when it came to airhead Zaza, you couldn't be certain of anything. Zaza had a heart of gold but really... Dottie frequently wondered whether she had anything between her ears. Cotton wool, most likely. Or blancmange.

Dottie scrutinised Zaza carefully. The presenter's eyes were red and puffy from crying and her mascara had smudged. Dressed in white pedal pushers and a black crop top, she looked a bit like a manic panda bear.

Dottie groaned. Zaza definitely needed to get her make-up done again – she couldn't possibly do a piece to camera in this state. It would give Didi even more ammunition against her.

At that moment Astoria was ushered into the room. Dottie glanced up, recognising her as the girl who'd shopped Max Harrison, then gestured to her to stand in front of the microphone.

'We'll be with you in a minute,' she said, before lowering her voice to address Zaza once more.

'Come on, Zaza. What's the problem? Has something dreadful happened?'

Astoria edged closer. This sounded interesting. She was intrigued to find out what was going on.

'It's... it's Didi,' wailed Zaza, her voice rising into an anguished sob. 'She's been horrible to me ...'

While Dougie Barton pretended to be busy, doodling multi-coloured crochets and quavers on his notepad,

Dottie rolled her eyes in exasperation. Really. Zaza was the biggest wimp she'd ever come across.

'Well, that's nothing new, is it?' she said briskly. 'What's she done this time?'

'She's, she's …'

Zaza was in such floods by now that she could scarcely get her words out.

'Come on, Zaza,' urged Dottie, irritation creeping into her voice. 'Spit it out.'

'She said that I'm next to useless and that the only reason Daniel's kept me on *Rise and Shine* is because he feels sorry for me. She said he's going to drop me at the end of the series.'

Dottie wanted to grab hold of Zaza and tell her not to be so flipping stupid. What was she like? The only way to treat Didi and her vicious tongue was to ignore everything she said. But did Zaza do that? Did she heck? She always took every horrible insult to heart.

Listening to all this, Astoria decided that this was the right moment to put in her pennyworth.

'Can I say something?' she said, her voice sounding uncharacteristically timid.

'Go on then,' said Dottie grudgingly.

'I think you're wonderful, Zaza. You're a much better presenter than Didi. Everyone at my school says so …'

Astoria's words were like music to Zaza's ears. In an instant she had stopped crying and was beaming at Astoria.

'Do they really?'

'They all say that you're far prettier. And you wear cooler clothes. And we don't think Didi should be so mean to you. Why *is* she so mean? I think she's just jealous …'

Dottie watched Zaza's face carefully. Surely she wasn't going to fall for a load of flannel from this girl? Astoria Lennox – with her sunflower yellow ra-ra skirt and blonde curls – looked all sweetness and light. But Dottie had seen the way she'd sneaked on that boy in the queue outside. *And* the ruthless manner in which she'd turned her back on her adoring parents. No, Astoria wasn't quite as ingenuous as she liked to make out.

But Astoria's adoration was precisely what Zaza longed to hear.

'What a delightful girl,' she murmured. She tilted her head towards Astoria, willing her to say more.

'It would be so much better if you presented the show by yourself…'

By this time Dottie had heard quite enough sucking-up for one day.

'Right,' she said, briskly taking charge. She knew no one else would. Dougie Burton was far too laid back and Zaza too clueless. 'Now. We'd better get on with the audition, hadn't we? We've got loads more contestants to see. Are you ready, guys? And Gloria, could you be a darling and touch up Zaza's make-up?'

A glamorous woman in four-inch stilettos and a scarlet trouser suit popped out from behind one of the vast curtains. Clutching what looked like a mini tool-kit, she hurried over to Zaza, expertly wiped the mascara from her cheeks and redid her eye make-up and lipstick. She stood back and examined her handiwork critically, then vanished behind the curtain as quietly as she'd appeared – just like the Fairy Godmother in *Cinderella*.

Dottie signalled to two young men in jeans lounging in the corner. They nodded back and ambled towards the camera at the far end of the studio. One grabbed hold of the camera prop while the other pulled on a pair of headphones and pointed the sound boom in Astoria's direction.

'OK, Astoria?' said Dottie. 'After three I want you to say who you are, your age and where you come from.

Then tell us what you're going to sing. Speak as loudly and clearly as you can. Right? On my count. One. Two. Three.'

Dottie had to hand it to Astoria. These stage kids knew what they were doing all right. Whereas some earlier contestants had been overcome by nerves – one girl had rushed out sobbing the minute she was asked a question – Astoria remained completely unfazed. She knew precisely what was required.

On the count of three, Astoria smiled straight into the camera and, without a trace of self-consciousness, said: 'Hello everyone. I'm Astoria Lennox. I'm twelve years old and I live in London. I'm going to sing my favourite song of all time – *Eternal Flame*. I hope you enjoy it.'

Within the first few bars of the old Bangles' hit, all three judges were utterly spellbound by Astoria's performance. It was flawless.

Dottie sped through the checklist Daniel had given her, ticking off each one in purple ink.

Singing – tick.

Dancing – tick.

Personality – tick.

Looks – tick.

Style – tick.

And so it went on, till the page was a scrawling mass of purple ticks. Dottie glanced over at Zaza's sheet. And at Dougie's. They had both given Astoria a firm thumbs-up too.

It was funny, reflected Dottie thoughtfully. She'd seen girls who could sing better that day, girls who could dance better, girls who were prettier – and girls who were a lot nicer. But – much as she hated to admit it – somehow Astoria had that extra special something that the others lacked … She had *star quality*.

6
Decision Time

DANIEL DREWSOME felt like tearing his hair out with exasperation. It was nearly midnight on Friday. There were less than nine hours till *Rise and Shine* went on air and the eight judges were still arguing over which contestants should go through to the Starspotter finals. For the hundredth time Daniel ran his fingers through his glossy, shoulder-length black hair and sighed heavily. They'd just about settled on three – two boys and a girl – but they simply couldn't agree on number four and number five. How were they ever going to come to a decision?

Daniel glanced round the room. Apart from the indefatigable Dottie – who was as bright-eyed and bushy-tailed as ever – everyone looked completely shattered. Worst of all, Didi was in even more of a filthy temper than usual. She kept insisting that she needed a good eight hours' beauty sleep in order to do the show, although Daniel knew perfectly well that she planned to whiz off to a showbiz party in Covent Garden. Meanwhile Zaza was so tired that she could barely string two words together. But that was hardly unusual for Zaza. Dougie Barton, the music producer, had crashed out on the floor with exhaustion, while choreographer Grace Graves – or GG as she was universally known – was snoozing peacefully in an armchair in the corner. GG had a fearsome reputation in showbusiness but now she looked a bit like the dormouse in *Alice in Wonderland*, sweetly curled up in a ball with a coat draped across her.

Despite the team's valiant efforts to complete the auditions as swiftly as possible, the judges hadn't seen the last contestants till seven-thirty on Thursday night.

The next morning, the team had turned up at the *Rise and Shine* studios to discuss who should go through to the final.

All the *Sooper Dooper* children's programmes had been trailing the Starspotter competition for days, promising clips of the auditions, profiles of contestants and the grand announcement of the five lucky winners live on air. Dottie had even organised a hot air balloon emblazoned with the words '*Rise and Shine* – Saturday. Nine a.m. Be there or be square,' to fly above London to promote the show.

Didi and Zaza had given interviews to all the national newspapers, although Didi had got more coverage because she'd been unable to resist slagging off Zaza. So instead of reports praising Starspotter to the skies, the papers had been full of headlines like *TV PRESENTERS AT EACH OTHER'S THROATS* and *THE RISE AND SHINE SHOUT-A-DAY SHOW*.

Daniel was fed up with the judges and their constant wrangling. The trouble was that everyone wanted somebody different to win. For instance GG was only interested in kids who could break-dance, while Didi invariably went for the ones dressed in the trendiest gear, regardless of whether they could sing a single note in tune. Zaza favoured the youngest contestants because they were sweet and usually liked her better than Didi and Dougie had a soft spot for anyone who'd performed anything by one of his boybands.

As the massive clock in the *Rise and Shine* planning room struck midnight, Daniel hammered on the table. The blow was so hard that all the coffee cups rattled on their saucers. The *Rise and Shine* producer glowered menacingly, then jabbed a pudgy finger at Zaza, Didi, Dougie Barton, GG and the rest.

'Don't you know it's rude to do that?' whinged Didi.

Another flash of annoyance crossed Daniel's face. He'd just about had enough of Didi for one day. She was really pushing her luck. If it wasn't for the fact that he needed her to front the show she'd be out on her ear.

'What?'

'Point at people.'

Yet again Daniel struggled to hold on to his temper.

'We're getting flipping nowhere like this,' he bellowed at everyone in the room. Zaza was so shocked that she visibly jumped in her seat. 'Now look, you bunch of cretins. You're completely useless. The best thing for you lot is to go home, get some kip and report back here for the show at six-thirty sharp. Zaza and Didi – we'll whisk you straight into hair and make-up then. The papers will want the pair of you on their front pages on Sunday – I want you on sparkling form. Got it?'

'That's a sheer impossibility for some people,' murmured Didi spitefully, stealing a sideways glance at her sidekick. Zaza, however, was too dozy to notice.

'And that means no arguments,' shouted Daniel. 'Understand?'

The judges got to their feet wearily and ambled towards the door.

'Are you going to make the final decision yourself then?' Dottie asked idly as she gathered all her papers together. She was still wearing the lime green *Rise and Shine* T-shirt she'd had on yesterday. She had unbraided her plaits and her hair looked as though she'd experienced a severe electric shock.

'Yep,' said Daniel grimly. 'But you can sit right down, Dottie. You're not going anywhere. I need your help. That lot couldn't organise a chimpanzees' tea party.

43

You've got more common sense than all of them put together.'

Dottie grinned at Daniel. The rest of the Starspotter judges were such a bunch of idiots that it wasn't quite the compliment it sounded.

'Righty-ho,' she said, plonking herself back on her chair again. 'It's nice to know I'm needed. So where the heck do we start?'

Daniel scratched his head. He couldn't believe that after all the months of planning that had gone into organising the Starspotter competition he only had a few hours to get the finalists sorted out.

'I don't know. There were so many kids at the auditions that it's hard to remember individual performances. And we haven't got time to run through the videos. What a fiasco. Why did we rush it like this? We should have given ourselves at least another week to choose who's going through.'

'Oh for goodness sake, Daniel, pull yourself together,' said Dottie. Daniel might be her boss, but at this moment he needed a bit of straight talking. 'We haven't got time for recriminations now.'

She leaned back and delved into the leather satchel lying at her feet.

'Blooming Nora, I'm sure I've got these pictures here somewhere,' she said. 'Ah yes. Here we go. Look at these.'

She dumped a couple of bulging brown A4 envelopes on the table. A mass of colour photographs spilled out all over the polished wooden surface.

'What are they for?' demanded Daniel tetchily. 'This is *not* the time to be showing me your holiday snaps, Dottie. I can tell you that for nothing.'

Dottie giggled.

'Very funny. But look a bit more carefully. Do you recognise anyone here? These are pictures of every contestant me, Gloria and Rose thought were any good. We might have missed a few but I don't think so.'

Daniel looked puzzled.

'What on earth are you talking about? And who are Gloria and Rose when they're at home?'

'Gloria's the *Rise and Shine* make-up artist, of course,' said Dottie. 'She's been in showbiz since she was knee-high to a grasshopper and she saw virtually everyone at the auditions.'

'And Rose? Who's she? I've never heard of her.'

Dottie gaped at Daniel. He really must live on another planet. How could he possibly have worked on *Rise and Shine* for two years and not have the foggiest idea who Rose was?

'Rose, the tea lady. Come on – you must know her. Don't you drink tea?'

To tell the truth Daniel only drank the occasional cup of hot water with a dash of lemon juice squeezed into it. But he did have a vague recollection of a cheery middle-aged woman in a red and white spotted headscarf dishing out tea and biscuits to the crew.

'Not often. But come on Dottie. We've got to get cracking. What have Rose and her tea trolley got to do with any of this? Or Gloria for that matter? You're driving me nuts.'

Dottie stared at her boss. For a man who was supposed to be in charge of *Rise and Shine*, he was remarkably dense sometimes.

'Don't you see? Between us, we saw every single contestant in London *and* Manchester. The three of us were chatting before the first audition and we reckoned it would be a brilliant idea to photograph the ones we thought were any good. To jog our memories really.'

Daniel didn't have a clue what Dottie was burbling on about but anything that helped whittle a couple of thousand Starspotter contestants down to five sounded good.

'Don't hang about then. Let's have a look.'

Leafing through the pictures, Daniel had to give credit to Dottie. The idea of snapping the best performers had been a brainwave. Within half an hour they had not only chosen the fourth finalist but had narrowed the fifth choice down to two youngsters – a boy called Flynn Sanders, from Reading, and Kate Barnsley, from Lancashire.

But after two hours of arguing Daniel and Dottie could *not* agree. The trouble was that Daniel, his voice hoarse by this time, was rooting for Flynn, while Dottie wanted Kate to go through.

'The lad's got a sensational voice,' croaked Daniel. 'And you should have seen the way he back-flipped across the stage. The girls will love him. Just think about it, Dottie. Wouldn't it be amazing if *Rise and Shine* discovered a new teenage pop idol? I can just see him on the front cover of *Heat* magazine.'

Dottie gazed at the picture of Flynn. Admittedly she hadn't seen him perform but she'd taken an instant dislike to the sulky-faced teenager gazing back at her. Flynn Sanders' head was shaved and he had a stud threaded through his left nostril. Back flips or no back flips he looked as if he would be a nightmare to deal with. In part, of course, her antagonism towards Flynn was fuelled by the fact that she wanted Kate to go through. She was *so* talented. Dottie still found it hard to believe that the delicate-looking youngster should have such a huge voice.

'She's very pretty,' admitted Daniel, staring at the picture of Kate that Dottie had pushed across the table. 'Let me think. Ah yes. I do remember her now. Sang *River Deep, Mountain High*, didn't she?'

46

'That's her,' said Dottie eagerly, pleased that Kate had made enough of an impression for Daniel to remember.

'Mmm. She's got a powerful voice for a kid of her age.'

'She certainly has. And she's got a sweet nature too. Which is more than you can say about some of the others. That ghastly Astoria Lennox for starters. Ugh. I know she's good but she gives me the creeps.'

But Daniel was miles away, trying to work it out. They'd already got two girls and two boys. So should they choose another girl or another boy? Flynn and Kate were poles apart in style. Flynn was a tough guy – mums and dads would loathe him with a passion, but Daniel was pretty sure kids would think he was cool. Kate, on the other hand, had a great voice ... But wasn't she just a bit *too* nice?

Daniel stretched his arms in the air and yawned. It was three in the morning and he was bushed. Who should they choose? All of a sudden he grabbed hold of both pictures and jumped to his feet.

'Get the details of the four we've chosen out of the file, will you, Dottie?' he said. 'I need their show reels and phone numbers so we can ring them live on the show.'

'And Kate's too?' said Dottie hopefully.

'Yep, all right. Get Kate's. And Flynn's. I want to think about it a bit more before we go on air.'

Dottie crossed her fingers behind her back.

'Please choose Kate,' she mouthed silently to herself. 'Please choose Kate ...'

She opened her mouth to plead Kate's case once more but it was too late. Daniel had gone.

7
And the Finalists Are...

DESPITE HER lack of sleep, Zaza Jones looked as fresh as a daisy. It was only eight-thirty but she'd already been through hair and make-up and was busy pulling on her *Rise and Shine* clothes. She smiled at her reflection in the mirror. Perfect. The wardrobe department had really come up trumps with her outfit today. They'd teamed a fluorescent yellow mini-dress with a matching hipster belt and knee-high boots. Zaza giggled to herself. The ensemble was a million times better than the boring old vest and jeans they'd given to Didi.

It was no accident that Zaza looked so sensational and Didi so dreary. The truth was that Didi had offended the wardrobe girls just once too often in recent weeks with all her sneering and sniping. In contrast, Zaza was always buying them flowers and sharing out her new lipsticks.

Five minutes later Dottie popped her head round the door to check whether Zaza and Didi were ready yet. At first she couldn't even spot them amid the chaos. The wardrobe department was situated in a tiny room at the back of the *Sooper Dooper TV* studios. There was hardly room to swing a cat, let alone store the countless clothes rails, mirrors, make-up boxes and hair-dryers Zaza and Didi needed.

For a split second Dottie panicked. Surely the girls couldn't have gone missing? Not on such an important day for the show. Even if they'd had another of their infamous spats they wouldn't do that. Would they?

48

Out of the blue Zaza peeped round a packed clothes rail and beamed at Dottie.

'Wotcha,' she giggled. 'This place would be great for playing hide and seek, wouldn't it?'

'Certainly would,' agreed Dottie. Zaza was so babyish sometimes that it was hard to believe she held down a top TV job. 'Only don't try it now – not unless you want to give me a heart attack, anyway. There's only thirty minutes to go till we're live on air.'

'Right you are, Dottie,' said Zaza, as first she and then Didi emerged from behind the clothes rail.

Dottie did a double take when she caught sight of Zaza's amazing dress. 'Hey, Zaza, you look fantastic. What a great colour. It's so zingy – it reminds me of lemon sherbet. Those sweets used to be my absolute favourites.'

'Thanks,' said Zaza. She did a twirl for Dottie's benefit.

Didi glowered as Dottie disappeared down the corridor. 'Charming,' she muttered. 'Don't say anything about my outfit then will you, Miss Snotty Dottie?'

'What did you say, Didi?' asked Zaza. 'I didn't quite catch…'

'Oh belt up. And save your Miss Goody Two Shoes act for the show, will you? You might pull the wool over Dottie's eyes but you certainly don't fool me.'

A hurt look appeared on Zaza's face. She genuinely didn't know what Didi was talking about.

'Hang on a mo,' said Didi suddenly. She'd just had an idea.

'What?'

Didi tried to look contrite.

'I'm sorry, Za. I shouldn't have said that. I didn't mean to hurt you. I'm a bit het up, that's all. It's a big day for *Rise and Shine* after all, isn't it?'

'I s'pose,' mumbled Zaza.

'I know,' said Didi. 'Let's get a coffee to calm ourselves down. Yes?'

Zaza looked doubtful. In general she tried not to drink too much coffee before the show. She was always terrified she might need a pee halfway through. But then again, she hated the frosty atmosphere that had built up between her and Didi over the past few weeks.

'Oh go on, then,' she agreed. 'Let's go and look for Rose and her tea trolley.

The two girls strolled down the corridor, peeping into each dressing room in turn. After several minutes of searching they finally found Rose in Daniel Drewsome's office.

Rose was busy pouring Daniel a pint-sized glass of hot water. She regarded him intently as she popped in a wedge of lemon, then handed him a fistful of digestive biscuits.

'You'll need these to keep your strength up, lovey,' Rose told him. 'Dottie says you've been up all night on this Starspotter caper.'

Daniel smiled wearily at the tea lady. He was having trouble keeping his eyelids propped open. And as for having the strength to bite into his biscuit, forget it.

'Right girls, what can I do for you?' said Rose briskly, turning towards Zaza and Didi. Her eyes popped out of her head when she saw Zaza's dress.

'Oh, I say. What a picture you look today, dear. That colour… well I never. It does suit you.'

The expressions on the two girls' faces said everything. While Zaza grinned fit to burst, Didi looked incandescent with rage. She'd just about had enough of Zaza getting all the compliments today. It really wasn't fair.

'Black coffees for both of you, is it?' asked Rose. She knew the beverage preferences of the entire *Sooper Dooper* staff so well that she could recite them in her sleep.

Zaza and Didi watched as the kindly tea lady poured hot coffee into two large *Rise and Shine* mugs.

Rose handed Zaza her mug first. She'd always had a soft spot for her.

'You're a superstar, Rose,' said Zaza appreciatively, lifting the mug towards her mouth to take a sip.

'It's a pleasure, dear…' began Rose. The tea lady broke off in horror as Didi inexplicably lost her balance and toppled against Zaza. The mug Zaza was holding flew out of her hands, spilling coffee all over her gorgeous yellow dress. Zaza screamed out in shock as the scalding coffee splashed down her front and all over the floor.

It was Rose who came to the rescue. Daniel was so transfixed by what had happened that he was unable to move, while Didi just kept staring at the ruined yellow frock. Rose grabbed a couple of tea towels from the top of her trolley and began frantically wiping away the coffee.

'Are you all right, dear?' she asked anxiously. 'Has it burned you?'

On the verge of tears, Zaza shook her head. In fact Rose had reacted so swiftly that the coffee hadn't managed to seep through her dress but it was still a shock.

'I'm f-f-fine,' she stuttered. 'But my dress … it's completely ruined. What am I going to do?'

Pulling himself together, Daniel took charge.

'Now, don't panic,' he instructed Zaza. 'Are you all right to carry on with the show?'

Zaza nodded.

'I think so. Yes.'

'Thank heavens for that,' said Daniel, full of relief. Zaza wasn't the bravest girl he'd ever come across. 'Now, go back to Wardrobe and get them to dig you out another outfit. And stay calm – you've got bucket-loads of time.'

Daniel glanced at his watch. This wasn't entirely true.

It was twenty minutes before the show went on air, but there was no point in stressing Zaza any more.

'And as for you,' he yelled, waving his fist in Didi's direction. 'How could you do that? She could have ended up in hospital because of you. She could have been horribly scalded, scarred even...'

Didi stared back at Daniel as if butter wouldn't melt in her mouth.

'Surely you don't think I...' she began.

'I absolutely do think so, yes,' he roared.

Didi's lower lip trembled theatrically.

'And you can stop that silly little act too,' raged Daniel. 'You were so jealous of all the compliments Zaza was getting that you had to throw a spanner in the works. You just had to go and spoil it. Didn't you?'

Didi opened her mouth to deny it, but before she could say anything Daniel started shouting at her again.

'Oh for goodness sake, don't waste my time with your pathetic excuses. Get out of my sight. I've had enough of you for one day. As if I didn't have enough on my plate without all this.'

Shaken by Daniel's tirade – and by the knowledge that he knew perfectly well what she'd done – Didi hurried off to get her make-up redone. She was in enough trouble for one day. She didn't want to be late.

Zaza's grey-blue eyes shone with excitement. She and Didi were sitting side by side on the famous spotty sofa, waiting for the Starspotter competition theme tune to finish. The show had begun with a report about the Masai Mara game reserve in Kenya, followed by a piece on how to grow ten-foot-high sunflowers. But now it was nine twenty-nine and the moment everyone had been waiting for with baited breath had finally arrived.

Zaza smoothed her dress over her legs. After the earlier

catastrophe with the coffee she was now wearing a sky blue mini-dress with lilac epaulettes and cuffs. It was almost as eye-catching as the yellow one. Not quite – although Zaza was pleased to note that it still looked an awful lot better than Didi's lacklustre vest and jeans. Ha ha ha, thought Zaza. It served Didi right for being so mean.

Watching the proceedings from the viewing gallery, Daniel observed the Starspotter graphics leap across the screen.

'Sixty seconds to go,' he warned Zaza and Didi through the tiny ear pieces they wore. 'Good luck, everyone.'

With ten seconds to go he counted the crew down.

'Ten, nine, eight, seven, six, five, four, three, two, one – and over to you, Zaza.'

With the camera trained directly on her pretty face, Zaza flashed the viewers a wide smile.

'The big moment's come at last,' she said. 'The whole nation is desperate to know who they are – the lucky five who've made it through to *Rise and Shine*'s Starspotter final...'

'And you're not the only ones – we can't wait either,' said Didi, grinning fit to burst. Deep down, she cursed herself, acutely aware that she'd come in a second too early. She had cut off the last word of Zaza's sentence in her rush to be heard.

'Don't rush your lines,' instructed Daniel brusquely through her earpiece. 'You've got plenty of time.'

'We've spent all week watching our amazing contestants perform onstage in London and Manchester,' continued Didi, reading her words off the autocue. 'You were all truly sensational, there's no doubt about it. But now comes the difficult part.'

'We've had to whittle the numbers down to five,' said Zaza.

'An impossible task,' said Didi. 'But someone had to do it.'

Up in the viewing gallery Daniel whirled round in his revolving chair and bellowed at Dottie.

'Clips ready to go, Dot?'

'Yep,' said Dottie. 'Ready when you are.'

Zaza winked at the camera, showing off her false eyelashes to full effect.

'But just to keep you in suspense just a teeny weeny bit longer we've got a real treat in store. So here's a look at some of the very best – and the very worst – performances we saw.'

Instantly a film of some of the London and Manchester auditions flashed up onscreen. They ranged from a young boy in a dapper suit and bow tie singing *Spirit in the Sky* in the wrong key to a girl with rainbow-coloured hair extensions performing a rap version of *Ave Maria*. In the main though, the singing was incredible.

'So that's just a taste of the amazing talent we've uncovered,' gushed Didi. 'I'm sure we'll be seeing loads of you in the Top Twenty in years to come. It'll be me and Zaza begging for your autographs rather than the other way round.'

'But now it's time to put you all out of your misery,' said Zaza. 'Can we have an extra-special fanfare?'

There was an ear-splittingly loud drum roll, followed by a cacophony of trumpets.

'Lovely,' said Didi, putting her hands over her ears and making a fake grimace for the camera. She waved a handful of gold envelopes in the air tantalisingly. 'Right. These are the names of our five sensational finalists.'

As she tore open the first envelope, the drum roll sounded again.

'Just like a grown-up awards ceremony, isn't it? Here goes. Finalist number one is – Tommy Brown. Tommy is thirteen-years-old, he's mad-keen on football and he comes from Leeds. Let's take a look at him strutting his stuff.'

As the tape of Tommy singing *What I Go To School For* blasted into the nation's living rooms, Dottie was busy dialling up the telephone number on Tommy's form. All the contestants had been asked to give a contact number where they'd be when the results were announced on Saturday morning so Zaza and Didi could talk to the lucky winners.

'Come on Tommy, pick up the phone,' muttered Dottie. 'Come on …'

8
Whoops of Delight

'RUN, TOMMY, run. You can do it, you can do it, lad. YESSSSS ....'

Tommy Brown's dad couldn't contain himself any longer. He punched the air in triumph. *Grove Park Wanderers: 1. Brookside Secondary: 0.* Words couldn't describe the way Brian Brown felt at seeing his son speed like the wind down the left wing and hammer the ball into the back of the net. Seconds later, the ref blew the whistle for half-time.

'Did you see that, love? Did you see that? Wasn't he magnificent? I've never seen anything like it. The boy's a natural. He could make a career out of this. You just watch him.'

Brian Brown swung round to his wife, expecting to see his own pride mirrored in her face.

But Sarah Brown's face was ashen. She looked as if her son had just been handed a red card, not scored a vital goal in the local school derby.

'You shouldn't get ...' she began. But it was too late. Brian Brown was already bounding up the pitch, desperate to slap Tommy on the back and congratulate the rest of the team for playing such a blinder.

'... him so worked up,' added Sarah Brown, her voice trailing away to nothing.

Seconds later Tommy detached himself from his team mates and his dad and ran up to her, a huge beam on his face. He was a tall, gangly boy with muddy knees and cropped blond hair. His cheeks glowed from the exertion of the match.

'Was I good – or was I good?' he yelled at her.

Despite her anxiety, Sarah Brown grabbed hold of Tommy and planted a huge kiss on his cheek. She'd never seen him look so happy.

'You were grand, lad,' she whispered. 'You were just grand.'

'Hey geroff, Mum, you'll show me up in front of my mates,' he said, wiping his face with a mud-spattered hand.

'Sorry, love. I couldn't help myself.'

Tommy was the youngest of Sarah and Brian Brown's four children. All the older kids had grown up and left home. The twins, eighteen-year-old Sinead and Scarlett, were at college in Leeds while seventeen-year-old Kevin had just joined the army.

So thirteen-year-old Tommy, the baby of the family, was the only one left. Perhaps this was why Sarah Brown wrapped him in cotton wool like she did. She hated seeing him get hurt. He'd broken his left ankle last season after a vicious tackle by an older boy and she couldn't bear it to happen again.

But there were two other reasons for Sarah's protect-iveness.

The first dated back to his babyhood. Tommy had been born with a hole in the heart and even though, just as the doctors had predicted, it had healed by itself within a year, Sarah still watched his health like a hawk.

The second was that football wasn't Tommy's only gift.

Tommy was a brilliant dancer. His older sisters had attended June Jordan's Dancing School down the road in Harrogate for years and loved teaching dance steps to their baby brother. By the time Tommy was five, it was clear he was a natural. So Sarah – ignoring her husband's protests that dancing was for wimps – had enrolled Tommy for lessons along with his sisters.

Up until two years ago, when he started at Grove Park Comprehensive, Tommy had loved it, excelling at ballet and tap. He'd even appeared in the chorus of *Joseph and the Amazing Technicolour Dreamcoat* at the Leeds Apollo one Christmas. But when his new pals discovered he took dancing lessons in his spare time, they'd teased him mercilessly.

Tommy begged his mum to let him stop. Not only was he getting grief from his mates, but the sessions often clashed with his Saturday morning soccer matches. And when the chips were down, soccer came first. By a long chalk.

Sarah Brown had had several sleepless nights before reluctantly agreeing to Tommy's request. She hadn't mentioned it to her husband – he'd never have understood – but in secret she'd dreamed of Tommy finding fame and fortune with his dancing.

So the lessons had stopped nine months ago. Tommy would never admit it in a million years but his mum knew he missed them. She'd watched the way he danced along the hall whenever there was music in the house. She'd spotted his feet tapping under the table when she put the radio on at breakfast.

Sarah glanced surreptitiously at her watch. Nine thirty-four. The Starspotter results must have been announced by now. She would have given anything to have watched them at home, but Tommy was desperate for both his parents to watch him play.

It had taken all Sarah's strength of will to drag Tommy to the Starspotter auditions in Manchester. In the end she'd only managed to get him there by promising to buy him a new Leeds United football strip. Sarah smiled dreamily. She had been so proud watching him up on-stage, singing and dancing his heart out …

58

At that moment, Sarah's mobile rang. She fumbled in her coat pocket for it. Who on earth could be ringing at this time on a Saturday morning?

'Hello,' she said, sounding more abrupt than she intended.

'Mrs Brown?' said a woman's voice.

'Yes. And who are…'

'It's Dottie Birch. From *Rise and Shine*. I've got some news for Tommy. Is he there?'

'You what?' Sarah Brown could scarcely believe what she was hearing.

'Can you get him?' said Dottie, her voice sounding more urgent.

'Has he …'

'Get Tommy,' ordered Dottie, frantic by this time. 'We need him on air. NOW.'

Sarah glanced across the pitch. Tommy was standing by the goal, surrounded by his school pals. They were all laughing and joking together, reliving the first half.

'Right,' said Sarah. 'I'll run as fast as I can.'

Sarah knew she must look a comical sight, a middle-aged woman in jeans and anorak tearing up the side of the pitch.

'Tommy,' she yelled breathlessly, thrusting her mobile at her son. 'Tommy. Quick. You've got a phone call.'

Tommy stared in bewilderment at his mum. Actually, it was more than bewilderment. He was beside himself with embarrassment. Here he was, in the middle of a crucial game, being ordered to take a phone call.

'Save it, Mum,' he hissed. 'Don't be soft. *I can't talk now.*'

But Sarah held her ground and refused to budge.

'You'll have to,' she said, once again shoving the phone at Tommy. 'Go on.'

A couple of Tommy's team mates were laughing openly at his discomfiture now.

'Who is it, pal?' said one of them. 'Yer girlfriend?'

Furious at being shown up like this, Tommy snatched the phone from his mum.

'What?' he yelled into the mouthpiece.

'It's Dottie Birch from *Rise and Shine*. I'm ringing with some great news. You're one of our Starspotter finalists. In thirty seconds time you'll be live on air to talk to Zaza and Didi.'

Tommy was so stunned that his legs crumpled beneath him. He couldn't make head or tail of what Dottie Birch was on about.

'Is this a wind-up?' he said finally.

'No it is not,' replied Dottie firmly. 'Now listen. Zaza and Didi are going to be asking you for your reaction shortly so can I give you a bit of advice?'

'Go on then.'

'Sound as if you're pleased. Thrilled even. D'you think you can manage that?'

After Tommy Brown's muted response, the *Rise and Shine* crew were praying that the other finalists might show a bit more enthusiasm. A few whoops of excitement wouldn't go amiss.

And luckily, that's precisely what they got. When Didi opened the second gold envelope, finalist number two turned out to be Sophy McBride, a fourteen-year-old from the island of Colonsay in the Hebrides. The moment Dottie put her on air, there was so much hollering and cheering in the background that Zaza and Didi could scarcely make out what the teenager was saying.

'So what's Colonsay like, Sophy?' asked Didi, trying to draw Sophy out.

'Very quiet,' Sophy shouted back.

'Certainly doesn't sound it.'

Sophy laughed. 'Well it is usually. It's a beautiful place

but it's mainly heather and sheep and sea. We're so far away from everywhere else that we only got a decent telly reception a few months back. We only used to have the radio.'

'It must have been quite a journey getting to Manchester for the auditions,' remarked Didi.

This was the understatement of the year. In fact it had taken Sophy ten hours to get to Manchester. The ferry ride from Colonsay to Oban was three hours alone and the car journey another seven. Sophy wouldn't have made at all if it hadn't been for the lucky fact that her dad had a fish delivery to take to Manchester. He'd driven her all the way to the Deansgate Theatre, deposited her in the queue and hared round the city delivering oysters, mussels and salmon to swanky restaurants. The van had stunk to high heaven of fish all the way there and back but luckily Sophy was used to it.

'Aye, it was that,' agreed Sophy, knowing better than to bore everyone rigid with the details.

'We've just shown the nation a clip of you singing your version of Nelly Furtado's *Fly like a Bird*,' said Zaza. 'Is she one of your favourite singers?'

'Aye,' said Sophy again. 'She's wicked. I'd give anything to sing like her. Or Joss Stone.'

'Well, you gave an ace performance and we can't wait to meet you pretty soon,' said Didi. 'At our secret hideaway in …'

'But we're not going to spoil the surprise,' giggled Zaza. 'Are we, Didi?'

Finalist number three was another boy – fourteen-year-old Scooter Mason, from Windsor, in Berkshire.

At the precise moment his name was announced, Scooter was sitting in his dad's office in the middle of Slough, bored out of his brain and totally oblivious to the fact that the Starspotter results were on TV.

The sky was grey and it had begun to drizzle with rain. Scooter sighed with frustration. Slough on a wet Saturday morning was *not* where he wanted to be. He wished his dad would hurry up and finish all his stupid work stuff. His saxophone lesson started at ten-fifteen and he couldn't miss it. He simply couldn't. The teacher had said Scooter's playing had come on in leaps and bounds recently and he might move him into his jazz group if he carried on like this.

Scooter's dad was a reporter for the *Daily Despatch*, one of the UK's best-selling tabloid newspapers. Bill Mason covered the whole of the South East, which was why he'd based himself in Slough. Scooter still couldn't work out what was so urgent that his dad had to come in on a Saturday. It was weird.

Scooter glanced around the empty office. His dad shared it with a sports guy and a reporter from the *Sunday Sentinel* and the place was a complete tip, even worse than his garden shed at home. And that was saying something. The desks were crammed to overflowing with telephones, computers and piles of old newspapers. The congealed remains of yesterday's lunch – a yucky Chinese takeaway by the looks of it – lay abandoned on one desk and endless empty coffee cups were strewn all over the place. Meanwhile Bill Mason was hunched over his desk, sort of whispering down the receiver. He'd been doing that for half an hour now, ringing endless police stations and asking funny questions about a woman called Polly Franzetti or something.

'Have you finished now, Dad?' yelled Scooter when Bill put the phone down for the umpteenth time.

'No, I have *not* finished now,' said Bill in a sharp voice. 'I've got a few more calls to make.'

Scooter groaned and kicked the wastepaper bin next to the desk where he was sitting. A load of crumpled paper spewed all over the carpet. He'd go mad if he had to sit around in this dump much longer. He'd have brought his PSP with him if he'd known his dad was going to make him wait this long.

'What's the matter, son?' Bill was obviously hanging on to speak to someone.

'I'm *bored*,' moaned Scooter, sounding like a whiny toddler.

Bill Mason banged on his desk with irritation. Scooter knew that any moment now his dad would launch into his usual diatribe. About how when he was a lad he didn't have half the things Scooter had and yet he'd never had any trouble amusing himself.

'When I was a lad I didn't have …' began Bill Mason.

'Half the things you've got, yeah, yeah, yeah,' mouthed Scooter without thinking.

Scooter caught his dad's eye and they both began to laugh.

'You cheeky monkey. Now look, I'll be finished here in ten minutes. I know it's tedious having to wait but… why don't you switch on the telly? It's over there, above the news desk.'

His face brightening, Scooter leapt up and moved across to the TV. Grabbing the remote, he deftly ran through the stations, rejecting everything as rubbish till he got to *The Rise and Shine Saturday Show*.

The sound of *Rise and Shine* blaring out of the telly at top volume made Bill Mason jump out of his seat.

He cupped his hand over the mouthpiece and bellowed across at Scooter.

'Turn that blasted thing down.'

His heart beating wildly – he didn't want to get on the wrong side of his dad again – Scooter repeatedly hit the remote, desperate to find the volume control. The buttons were so well-used and worn that the arrows and numbers had been rubbed away. Several seconds passed before his fingers punched the right one.

Scooter's dad stuck a thumb in the air and grinned.

Scooter grinned back. His dad was all right really. A bit hot-tempered now and then – and he wished he'd spend less time at the pub with his reporter mates and more time at home with him and his little brother Teddy. But not bad considering.

All of a sudden, Scooter sat bolt upright. He couldn't believe what he was hearing. Zaza and Didi were in the middle of announcing the Starspotter results. Scooter hadn't expected them for weeks yet.

Bill Mason slammed the phone down with a flourish and leaned back in his chair. At last he was getting somewhere with his inquiries.

'Anything good on?' he asked his son.

'Ssh Dad, this is important,' said Scooter.

'Doesn't look very fascinating. Those two girls are a right shower, aren't they?'

At that very moment a young boy appeared onscreen. He had short spikey red hair, a mass of freckles and a mischievous expression. He wore a T-shirt with Che Guevara's face on it and a pair of baggy olive green combats.

Mesmerised by the screen, for once Bill Mason was lost for words.

'What? What the blazes …? How …?'

'I don't believe it,' Scooter muttered under his breath.

'It's you,' spluttered Bill finally. 'What the heck's going on? What on earth are you doing on the telly?'

Before Scooter could half-begin to answer, the boy on the telly began to sing. He gave a rendition of Smokey Robinson's *Tracks Of My Tears* that was so perfect that Bill Mason had to swallow hard.

The pair of them watched in silence, dumbstruck by

the youngster's performance – Scooter because he was actually ON TV, his dad because he'd had no idea his son could sing like that.

'And that's finalist number three,' screeched Zaza as the clip faded out. 'Scooter Mason.'

'I did it, I did it,' yelled Scooter, jumping up and down. 'I've made it into the Starspotter final. Wow.'

'Scooter,' said Zaza, an unusually serious look appearing on her face. 'If you're watching then please give us a call. We've tried to get you on the number you gave us, but it's permanently engaged and we don't seem to be able to get through. Come on – we want to talk to you. The nation wants to talk to you.'

Typical, thought Scooter. His mum was such a chatterbox on the phone. She was probably burbling away to Auntie Margie, as usual. The two sisters never discussed anything important but they phoned each other at least twice a day.

'What *is* going on?' demanded Bill yet again. 'Why are you on the telly? What's it all about? What's Starspotter when it's at home?'

Scooter stared at his dad in amazement. Bill Mason was a reporter – forever boasting that he had his finger on the pulse. He must have heard of the Starspotter competition. What planet had he been on all week?

Scooter took a deep breath. He'd better start at the beginning.

'*Rise and Shine* is a children's TV show,' he explained. 'They've launched a talent show. For singers and dancers between eleven and fourteen. They held an audition in London last week. Well a couple of days ago, actually. And I … I …'

'You went to it,' said Bill, finishing Scooter's sentence for him. 'Where was it? How did you get there? Why didn't you tell me and your mum?'

Scooter scratched his head pensively. If this was how his dad operated at work, bombarding people with questions, he was amazed anyone told him anything.

'It was a spur of the moment thing,' he said. 'Me and Matt went together. We thought it would be a laugh. We queued up on our way back from collecting our tickets for the Arsenal–Spurs game.'

Scooter and his best pal Matt were big Arsenal fans and Bill often managed to wangle them tickets to home games from the *Despatch* sports desk.

'And what's the prize?' asked Bill. 'Will me and your mum be able to retire on the proceeds?'

Scooter laughed. He could tell from his dad's tone of voice that he wasn't cross. Far from it. In fact he sounded quite impressed by Scooter's initiative.

'Not quite yet,' said Scooter. 'But you never know. They're choosing five finalists and they're going to give us coaching and turn us into stars. A bit like *Fame Academy*, I think. Or *Pop Idol*.'

'Well you'd better get on the blower then, hadn't you? Or do you want me to do it for you?'

'You do it,' said Scooter, suddenly feeling nervous.

Bill flicked through his dog-eared contacts book. Within seconds he had found the number of *Sooper Dooper TV* and was through to the switchboard. That was the good thing about having a news reporter as a dad, thought Scooter. He might work terrible hours, evenings and weekends and things, but he had the telephone numbers of loads of important people. Scooter had looked through his dad's precious contacts book once and spotted that he had numbers for the Pope, the Prime Minister *and* Buckingham Palace. He was dead impressed.

'I thought you reckoned pop music was a waste of space these days, Scoot,' said Bill as he waited for the switchboard to answer the phone.

Scooter shrugged.

'Not all of it, Dad,' he mumbled.

The truth was that Scooter had always excelled at singing. He'd been in the school choir for yonks, loved doing Elvis impersonations in the bath and all that. The only drawback was that his voice had broken last year and he'd got a bit self-conscious.

But this term Mr Wheatley, the new music teacher at school, had changed everything. Out of the blue he'd made all the Year Nines sing a bit from the musical *Fame*. Solo as well. Everyone had been cringing about it and saying they couldn't do it. But as soon as Scooter stood up and opened his mouth to sing *I'm Gonna Live Forever*, his nerves and embarrassment just melted away into thin air. He'd actually enjoyed it – and judging from the beatific look on Mr Wheatley's face and all his mates' grins, they had too.

'That was delightful, John,' said Mr Wheatley, scribbling furiously in his notebook when Scooter sat down. 'Delightful.'

Scooter beamed. He could forgive Mr Wheatley anything for that remark. Even for calling him John.

Scooter had been called Scooter for as long as he remembered. Well, his parents had christened him John. But his dad had started calling him Scooter when he started walking – because of the way his elder son always scooted about. The name just stuck – and now most people had forgotten that Scooter's real name was John. All the teachers called him Scooter too, even the headmaster. But Mr Wheatley was new this term so maybe he didn't realise how much Scooter hated being called John.

Scooter stared back at his dad, aghast at what he'd just said. Did he have any idea? Of course he didn't think music was a waste of space. Well, he might have said so a few times. But it was only when he thought his voice was rubbish. He'd give his right arm to be a famous singer when he grew up – a kind of mixture between the Arctic Monkeys and Liam Gallagher maybe. Now that would suit him fine. Just fine.

'Hello,' bellowed Bill down the phone. 'Is that *Rise and Shine*? I think you want to talk to my son. Scooter Mason.'

9

The Kidstars' Kid

THE NINE a.m. ballet class at Kidstars had never seen anything quite like it.

One moment Madame Tbliski was instructing her twenty most able pupils, all clad in electric blue leotards and matching legwarmers, as they practised their pliés at the barre. The next, all hell let loose.

Madame Tbliski was a tall, elegant woman in her early fifties. She had jet-black hair scraped back in a severe bun and always wore an immaculately cut black leotard, a flowing ballerina skirt made of black tulle and black silk ballet shoes. She spoke in a thick Russian accent, although the rumour flying around Kidstars was that she actually came from Scunthorpe and wasn't Russian at all.

'Bend and stretch. Watch ze knees, Olivia. You must remember to bend, like zeez ...'

Only Madame Tbliski never got to the end of her sentence. She was halted in mid-flow by a huge commotion outside the class. First came shouting, then a massive crash, as a middle-aged man burst through the oak doors and into the hall. The doors catapulted open with such force that he was flung through the air, arms and legs flailing all over the place. He hit the parquet floor with a massive thud, landing flat on his back in an untidy heap in front of Madame Tbliski.

Madame Tbliski's master class consisted largely of girls, with a few boys dotted here and there. Far from being alarmed or frightened by this bizarre entrance, most of them burst into fits of giggles. Apart from Astoria Lennox, that is. She gazed in horror at the man, who was now scrambling to his feet.

How could he embarrass her like this? How could he? *And* he hadn't even bothered to get dressed properly. He looked a complete imbecile in his scruffy joggers and trainers. Oh, the shame of it. She was never going to live this down.

Madame Tbliski stared at the man coldly. She couldn't put her finger on it but he looked oddly familiar.

'What do you theenk you are doing?' she demanded icily, drawing herself up to her full 5ft 10ins. 'I weel not stand for eet. We are very busy rehearsing our end of year show. We cannot countenance interruptions like zeez...'

Her pupils stood in silence, trying to hide their laughter behind their hands. Astoria closed her eyes for a second, praying that this was a horrible dream and she would wake up soon. Sadly it was all too real. When her eyes flicked open again her father was still standing there.

'I'm, I'm sorry, miss,' said Denis. He shuffled his feet awkwardly.

'It eez Madame,' snapped back Madame Tbliski.

Her sternness merely served to make Denis even more nervous and bumbling. He could cope with a few hundred rowdy hecklers at the Streatham Hippodrome but they were nothing compared to Madame Tbliski. She was far scarier than the toughest audiences he had to contend with. And that was saying something.

'Sorry, M–m–madam.'

'Madame,' corrected Madame Tbliski again.

'Whatever. I ... I ... Well, I w–w–wondered if I could have a word with our Astoria,' he stuttered.

'Eez it urgent?' demanded Madame. 'How do you say? Life and death?'

'Y–y–yes, it is. Life and death – that just about describes

it. You see I've had a telly company on the phone. They need to speak to Astoria now.'

'What? Right at zeez minute? It eez most irregular.'

All of a sudden a light flashed on inside Astoria's head. She knew what was happening. *Rise and Shine*. It had to be something to do with *Rise and Shine*. In all the excitement of the auditions she'd completely forgotten to ask when the finalists would be announced. They must have been so impressed that they didn't want her to slip through their fingers.

Summoning up every ounce of charm she possessed, Astoria skipped daintily up to Madame Tbliski.

'I'm so sorry about my father,' she said, her voice full of sweetness and light. 'I really don't want to disrupt the class any further so shall I take him outside and find out what all this is about?'

'That eez a good idea,' glowered the ballet teacher. 'But don't theenk zat zeez is ze end of ze matter. I cannot have my lesson being interrupted like zeez. Now, ze rest of ze class, back to work.'

The instant Astoria was out of the hall she turned on her father in a fury.

'Why did you have to show me up like that?' she yelled. 'Madame will have it in for me from now on. And I was hoping for the main part in the end of year show…'

Denis tried to calm his daughter down.

'Hush now, sweetheart,' he soothed, wrapping his arms around her in a huge bear hug. 'That's the least of your worries right now. We've had a call, darling. From *Rise and Shine*.'

'What did they say?' demanded Astoria. She could feel her heart beating fit to burst.

'They want to talk to you.'

'Well what are we waiting for then?' shrieked Astoria. 'Where's the number?'

Denis took a clunky-looking mobile out of his track suit pocket – Astoria had the latest mini-sized model of course but he couldn't afford one for himself – and fumbled for the scrap of paper he'd written the *Rise and Shine* number on.

'Hurry up, Dad. Honestly. You're so hopeless. If someone shouted "Fire!" you wouldn't run.'

Most fathers would have lost their temper at this point but Denis patiently continued sorting through all the screwed-up tickets and receipts he had stuffed in his pocket. Finally he produced the right one and dutifully began punching in the *Rise and Shine* number. He had to have a couple of goes at it before he got it right.

'Here, Dad, give it to me,' said Astoria, snatching the phone from Denis. 'Hello? Is that *Rise and Shine*? Good. It's Astoria Lennox here. I understand you want to talk to me. Well, here I am.'

The tension was building in the *Rise and Shine* studio. Tommy, Sophy and Scooter, reflected Daniel from his chair in the viewing gallery. Three finalists down, two to go.

'And now we come to finalist number four …' yelled Zaza, 'What can we tell you about her? Well, she's twelve years old, she's from Streatham in South London and she's… ASTORIA LENNOX. Give it up for Astoria.'

Dottie rolled her eyes at the mention of Astoria's name. She'd known since the auditions that Astoria was a dead cert for the final, but it still made her fume. She'd rarely met such a spoilt, self-centred girl in her life.

'Hi Astoria,' bellowed Didi into the phone. 'So what do you think about being one of our five Starspotter finalists? Surprised?'

'Really surprised,' said Astoria modestly. 'The other kids were so talented… I didn't think I stood a chance against them … I feel very very lucky.'

Chatting quietly to a couple of the sound engineers, Dottie choked on her words. Had Astoria Lennox just had a personality transplant or something? Was this really the Astoria Lennox who had been so full of herself? Who had sneaked on one of her fellow contestants and dumped her poor parents in a flash?

'Blooming Nora,' she muttered beneath her breath. 'Can someone pass the sick bucket? I think I'm going to be ill.'

Down in the studio below, Zaza and Didi were totally oblivious of Dottie's antipathy towards Astoria Lennox.

As a video clip of Astoria's performance at the auditions played to the nation, Zaza leaned over and whispered to Didi.

'Lovely girl, that. You mark my words – she's a real star in the making. Not nearly so big-headed as the others. I knew she'd make it.'

Daniel Drewsome glanced at the huge studio clock. The minutes were flying by at an alarming speed. It was nine-forty-five already – they'd better get a move on and announce the fifth and last finalist.

'You got number five all cued up?' he bellowed across to Dottie. She was talking nineteen to the dozen on her mobile and looking more and more anxious by the second.

'That's impossible,' she snapped at whoever she was talking to. 'He can't have. We only saw him at five-thirty on Thursday and he was on top of the world. What on earth was he thinking of? How could he be such a dur-brain? He's completely ruined his chances, you know. We can do loads of things at *Rise and Shine* but we can't get him out of a mess like that. Not when the police are involved. It would be really bad PR for the show.'

'*DOTTIE*,' roared Daniel. '*QUIT CHATTING,*

WILL YOU? I need number five in about ninety seconds. What are you playing at?'

'*FINE*,' yelled Dottie down the phone. 'And tell him not to come bellyaching back to us next week. He's completely blown his big break. Big time.'

'Can you please tell me what on earth is going on, Dottie?' demanded Daniel. 'And where the blazes is Flynn Sanders? We need him on the line double-quick.'

'Well, you can't have him,' snapped Dottie bad-temperedly. 'The stupid boy only went and grabbed a couple of paint cans on the way home from the auditions and sprayed graffiti all down the wall of Strawberry Hill tube station. He was picked up by the police and he's down to appear at the North London Youth Court at ten on Monday morning. His dad's just told me the whole story. He's none too pleased himself. Apparently it's not the first time he's done it.'

Daniel's face went pale. The show had gone so smoothly up till this moment – now it was threatening to collapse around his ears.

'Quick,' he roared at Dottie. 'Get hold of the other one. There's no time to waste. Get hold of her *NOW*.'

Kate Barnsley plucked a stray thread from the tatty red sofa. Her mum, sitting beside her, was poring over the whopping great electricity bill that had just arrived in the post and trying not to fret about how she was going to pay it.

Linda Barnsley was a very bad liar. Whenever she attempted to lie about anything – which wasn't very often – her face went bright red and she started to stutter. As a result she didn't tell fibs very often, but for once in her life dishonesty had prevailed this morning. Against all her instincts, she had run round to the newsagents at the crack of dawn and lied through her teeth, telling Gwenda

Graham that poor Kate was sick and couldn't possibly do her paper round. Gwenda, bless her, had been ultra-sympathetic – which only made Linda feel worse.

By the time Zaza and Didi had announced the fourth Starspotter finalist, Kate's heart was in her boots. She felt so cast-down that she figured she might as well be pedalling through the streets of Gribblesdale shoving papers through letter boxes. What a fool she'd been. How could she possibly have thought she stood a chance against the likes of Astoria Lennox? Girls like Astoria were steeped in showbiz. Astoria had the word *STAR* printed right through her like a stick of Blackpool rock.

'You all right, love?' said Linda. She gave Kate's slender arm a quick squeeze. Looking at her glum face, it was patently obvious she wasn't.

Kate shot her mum a wide, brave smile.

'Course.'

'Really?'

'Yes, Mum. Really.'

On screen Zaza and Didi were on the verge of announcing the name of the fifth winner. There was clearly some sort of delay – either that or Zaza was having one of her customary wobbles – because out of the blue Didi suddenly announced they were going to show a clip of the latest Jack Johnson video.

'Just to show you budding superstars how it is done,' giggled Zaza. 'Take it on down, Jack.'

'I wonder who the last finalist's going to be?' said Kate, snuggling up to her mum and trying to sound as if she couldn't care less.

Linda squeezed her hand so hard that Kate winced.

'Come on. Don't give up hope. It could be you, sweetheart. You're just as good as the ones who've got through. Your voice is much better than that Astoria girl. Hers grates a bit, don't you think?'

Kate knew her mum was trying to be kind so she nodded weakly.

Their discussion was interrupted by the sound of ferocious banging on the front door. Kate and Linda glanced at each other.

'Who's that at this hour on a Saturday morning?' said Linda.

'How do I know? I haven't got X-ray vision.'

For a second Linda was inclined to ignore the door but her kind heart swiftly got the better of her and she forced herself to her feet. She was worried that old Mrs Tate from next door might be in trouble. Mrs Tate was well into her eighties and she'd been having gip with her arm for a couple of weeks now.

When Linda opened the door Mrs Tate was indeed standing there, dressed in her customary overall, headscarf and bedroom slippers. But far from looking frail and elderly, she was in the rudest of health.

'Quick, quick, Linda love.' Mrs Tate was practically jigging up and down on the front step with excitement.

'You what?' Linda didn't have the first idea what Mrs Tate was on about.

'Quick. Get your Kate round to mine. There's a lass on the phone wants to speak to her. Says she's from the telly.'

Completely baffled by Mrs Tate's garbled message, but vaguely remembering that Kate had given the old lady's telephone number to *Rise and Shine*, Linda dashed into the sitting room and hauled Kate from the sofa. Kate, gripped by the Jack Johnson video, protested loudly, but Linda took no notice. She forcibly bundled her out of the house and straight round to Mrs Tate's.

'What are you doing, Mum?' said Kate irritably, trying to loosen her mum's grip. 'I was really enjoying that song. You know he's one of my favourites. Can't you wait for a second? I don't want to miss it.'

'Get on with you, love. Mrs Tate says you've got a phone call.'

'Who from?'

'The telly.'

'No,' said Kate, her eyes opening wide in shock. 'What do they want?'

'If you'd just get on that blinking phone you'd find out,' said Linda.

Kate felt like she was dreaming. She ran into Mrs Tate's brown and white tiled hall and picked up the old lady's old-fashioned telephone receiver.

'Hi,' she said softly. 'It's Kate here. Kate Barnsley.'

At the other end of the line, Dottie almost fainted with relief.

'Thank goodness for that. I thought you'd done a runner or something.'

'Why would I do that?'

'I dunno,' said Dottie. 'I thought you might have second thoughts.'

'Second thoughts,' said Kate. 'About what?'

'About the Starspotter competition of course. You've made it. You're in the final. Didi and Zaza will be speaking to you in about ten seconds. Are you OK with that?'

Stunned by Dottie's announcement, Kate felt her legs give way beneath her. She sank to the floor in disbelief.

'I don't believe it,' she murmured. 'I just don't believe it.'

'Believe what?' Straining to hear what Dottie was saying, Linda was desperate to know what was going on.

'I'm in the final, Mum,' whispered Kate. Then as the news slowly sank in, she shouted at the top of her voice: 'Can you believe it? *I'VE MADE IT. I'M IN THE FINAL …*'

10
Dottie's Posse

A SHIVER OF apprehension ran down Dottie's spine as the train drew nearer Penrith. In the last two hours the scenery had changed from straggly urban sprawl into a wild, hillier landscape. Astoria, who rarely ventured to the countryside if she could possibly help it, gasped in horror.

'I hope you're not going to force us to go for walks all the time,' she muttered to Dottie. 'You're not, are you? Because I won't go.'

'A few hearty mountain walks will do you the world of good,' smiled Dottie. 'Get some colour into those pale city cheeks of yours.'

Astoria winced and went quiet. She couldn't work out whether Dottie was kidding or not. She must be. Surely the *Rise and Shine* crew wouldn't risk taking them up a mountain. One of them might fall down a ravine and break a leg – and then where would the programme be? Dottie *must* be joking.

Dottie had drawn the short straw this time all right. How had she got landed with the task of nannying a load of kids at a house in the middle of nowhere? Trickier still was the fact that none of them had anything whatsoever in common. Apart from a desperate yearning to be pop stars, that is.

It was all Daniel Drewsome's fault. As per usual. At the umpteenth planning meeting for the Starspotter finals, the volatile *Rise and Shine* producer had dreamed up yet another brainwave.

'Got it,' he'd shouted, banging his fist on the table. 'We need one of the team to stay in the house with the kids. Y'know, to keep an eye on them, make sure they're on the straight and narrow. Be their big sister, if you like.'

'I'll be with them for the first couple of days,' Dottie had reminded him. 'And they won't be short of people to talk to with all the dance instructors, voice coaches and personal tutors hanging around. Isn't that enough? The place is going to be busier than Piccadilly Circus the rate you're going.'

Daniel's eyes had narrowed thoughtfully.

'No. We definitely need someone from *Rise and Shine* there too. Someone who'll keep their ear to the ground. And not just for a night or two. We need someone on site for the next ten days.'

'How about Zaza?' Dottie had suggested. 'I know she's a bit scatty but she's got a heart of gold.'

'Are you off your rocker, girl?' roared Daniel. 'Zaza Jones is a complete dipstick. She'd lose the lot of them in ten seconds flat. She'd need more looking after than the kids. No, Dottie. No way.'

'Well, who else is there?' said Dottie. 'You can't send Didi. She's more like the wicked stepmother than a big sister.'

'That's for sure,' agreed Daniel. 'No, it's got to be you, Dottie. You're the only one up to the job. The only one I can trust. But you'd better get cracking. There's no time to waste. Cancel everything in your diary for the next ten days. I want you there 24/7.'

Sure enough, the journey up to the Lake District had been a foretaste of what was to come. Dottie had arrived at Euston station bright and early, dressed in a *Rise and Shine* T-shirt and matching baseball cap, ready to meet Scooter and Astoria, the two London finalists. Her bag was stuffed to bursting with everything the kids might possibly need on the journey – drinks, sweets, snacks, paper, pens, travel Monopoly, plasters, travel sickness pills. Dottie congratulated herself – Mary Poppins herself couldn't have done a better job.

First to pitch up at Platform Five was an embarrassed-looking Scooter. He was accompanied by his dad, a short, stocky man in an ill-fitting charcoal suit.

'Aren't you going to tell her who you are, lad?' Bill Mason prompted Scooter.

The boy hopped awkwardly from one trainer-clad foot to the other. He was a good-looking boy, with spiky red hair and a mass of freckles – completely different from his father.

'Er, I'm Scooter,' he mumbled to Dottie.

'Yep, I remember you from the auditions,' said Dottie, trying desperately to put him at his ease. Blooming heck, if the boy couldn't cope with this bit, how was he going to manage in the Starspotter Academy?

Bill Mason then proceeded to bombard Dottie with a million and one questions about precisely where the Starspotter Academy was, how many staff there'd be and what the other finalists were really like. He even produced a battered notebook from his back pocket to jot everything down.

'Hang on, hang on,' said Dottie, interrupting Mr Mason in mid-flow. 'You know I can't give anything away. It's all top secret. Daniel Drewsome will have my guts for garters if I spill the beans now.'

At that moment Astoria Lennox arrived, flanked by her mum and dad. Denis Lennox was wheeling a trolley laden with more luggage than Dottie and Scooter put together, while Giselle anxiously checked through the Sainsbury's carrier bag she was holding.

'Bourbon biscuits,' she muttered to herself. 'Fanta Fruit Twist. Crisps. Kiwi fruit …'

Astoria looked as though she had spent hours getting ready. She wore a scarlet mini kilt, cropped denim jacket and striped red and white tights. Her long blonde hair had been teased into masses of tiny corkscrew curls cascading down her back. Dottie reckoned Astoria's mum must have been up all night doing that lot.

Denis and Giselle Lennox barely had time to introduce themselves before Astoria airily promised to send them a postcard when she got to the Starspotter Academy and waved them off.

'You won't forget, darling, will you?' said Giselle. 'We'll be anxious to know you've arrived safely.'

Meanwhile, as Scooter cringed in the background, Bill Mason was still firing off questions at all and sundry.

'And where do you come from, love?' he demanded of Astoria.

That did it. Dottie lost her temper.

'Will you stop asking your nosy parker questions and leave the contestants alone?' she yelled.

Honestly. As if she didn't have enough to cope with making sure she didn't lose anyone *and* lugging Astoria's endless pieces of matching red luggage on to the train. That last suitcase had been so heavy that Dottie had had to yell for a porter. 'Blooming Nora, this feels like a ton of bricks, Astoria. What on earth have you got in here?'

Irritated at being fobbed off in such a perfunctory fashion, Bill Mason carried on with his questioning.

'Surely you can at least tell me where my lad's going? I won't be able to sleep for worrying otherwise. He's barely been away from his mum and dad before. He might be homesick.'

Scooter's face flushed again. What on earth was his dad on about? Not able to sleep, indeed. Barely been away from his mum and dad. Homesick. Anyone would think he was a baby – not a strapping lad of fourteen.

'Look, Mr Mason,' snapped Dottie. 'I'm not being difficult, I'm really not. But you've already agreed to the terms of the competition. You signed reams and reams of paper last week giving permission for Scooter to spend the next ten days at the Starspotter Academy. You can't pretend you didn't.'

To her relief, Bill Mason had grinned and put his notebook away.

'Well you can't blame a chap for trying, love, can you? Not to worry. The paper's running a piece on the lad tomorrow anyway. I can just see the headline now. *My boy's first step to stardom.*'

Scooter's face had paled.

'No, Dad, you wouldn't …'

'Wouldn't I?' grinned Bill Mason. 'And there's a cute picture of you at the age of two in a romper suit. You'll love it.'

Dottie wasn't sure whether Scooter's dad was kidding or not. But Scooter should know – and the boy clearly believed him. When the time came to say goodbye to his father Scooter turned on his heel with a scowl and stomped off down the platform. Meanwhile Bill Mason had turned his attention to Astoria once more, grilling her for interesting snippets of information about herself. Fuming, Dottie grabbed hold of Astoria's hand and marched her on to the train.

'Really,' she muttered crossly to herself. Bill Mason had the hide of a rhinoceros. How did Scooter put up with him?

Daniel Drewsome was well-known in the TV business for keeping a tight rein on the *Rise and Shine* purse strings. True to form he had refused to splash out on First Class seats for Dottie and the Starspotter finalists.

Shocked by his dad's disclosure that his toddler pictures were going to be splashed all over the following day's

Daily Despatch, Scooter barely uttered a word on the long journey up north. This was in marked contrast to Astoria, who didn't draw breath. She recounted every detail of the parts she'd played in recent Kidstars productions, right down to the costumes she'd worn and her most show-stopping songs. She offered several bemused passengers her autograph and jumped into the aisle to demonstrate a few of her very best dance steps. She was just getting into her stride when the guard bustled down the carriage and told her off for causing an obstruction.

Astoria's antics took them as far as Manchester, where Kate and Tommy boarded the train. Enthused at the prospect of a fresh audience, Astoria launched into her triumphs all over again.

Dottie was thankful that Kate and Tommy were far easier to deal with than the London pair. Kate had greeted Dottie with a huge hug while Tommy grinned broadly and shook hands with everyone.

'I thought there were going to be five of us,' Kate said as she plonked herself next to Astoria. 'That's what Didi and Zaza said on the show, didn't they? Or have I got it wrong?'

'No, you're right,' said Dottie. 'But Sophy, our fifth finalist, lives in Scotland so she's meeting us at Penrith. I hope you'll like her. She's quite a character.'

Nothing had prepared Dottie and her charges for the sight that greeted them at Penrith station. As the train slowed to a halt, they saw scores of photographers and cameramen jostling for space on the platform. Even the streetwise Dottie was pole-axed. She'd been expecting a *Rise and Shine* crew to capture their arrival … but nothing like this.

As Astoria, Scooter, Tommy and Kate stepped from the train, flash bulbs exploded from every direction. Click. Click. Click. Click … the cameras went on and on.

The reactions of the Starspotter finalists were fascinating to watch. Astoria, who was accustomed to having her picture taken at Kidstars, flicked her hair back and gave a megastar smile. Scooter, who'd been to photocalls with his dad, grinned laconically while Tommy looked simply amazed by the stir they'd caused. But poor Kate was scared out of her wits. She'd never seen anything like it in her entire life. She felt so out of her depth that she took cover behind Dottie.

'How come there are only four kids?' bellowed a beefy reporter in a suit so crumpled that it looked as though he had slept in it.

'Have you lost one of them already?' yelled another. 'Now that would be a cracking story.'

Dottie grimaced. Little did the reporters know it but losing a Starspotter finalist was her worst nightmare.

'No, I have not lost any of them,' she said through clenched teeth. 'And if you lot would just shut up and move out of the way I might be able to get on with meeting the fifth contestant.'

'And then can we have all five in the line-up?' asked one of the photographers.

Dottie hesitated. Daniel hadn't said anything about doing a photocall in the middle of Penrith station. But what the heck. It would be good publicity for the show.

'OK,' she said. 'But you'd better make it snappy.'

At that moment Dottie spotted Sophy McBride hovering in the waiting room with her dad. Wow. She'd forgotten how striking Sophy was. The girl must be about 5ft 10ins tall, with long black dreadlocks and legs that went on forever. Sophy had told her at the Manchester auditions how she'd spent the first few years of her life in Jamaica. Her mum was Jamaican and her dad British and they'd moved to the remote Scottish island of Colonsay when she was five. Her dad had been born and bred there and now worked as a fisherman. Together with her parents and two younger brothers Sophy lived in a crofter's cottage overlooking the bay.

'Over here, Sophy,' shouted Dottie. 'Quickly. They need you in the picture.'

Sophy dumped her case at her dad's feet and ran to join the others. Tommy, Scooter and Kate arranged themselves in an awkward group behind Astoria, who was clearly loving every bit of the attention.

'Right,' said Dottie, taking charge of the line-up. 'You look a bit higgledy-piggledy like that. Let's get you sorted out. Sophy and Tommy, you're the tallest, so you'd better stand at the back. Then we'll have Kate in the middle, flanked by Astoria and Scooter.'

'Hey, that's not fair,' complained Astoria, miffed at Dottie for moving her from centre stage. 'Why should Kate be in the middle?'

'Well, you'll have to lump it. It's the best I can do right now. I don't want to be here all day. Now come on everyone, big smiles. Say c-h-e-e-s-e.'

11

The Starspotter Academy

IT WAS four p.m. by the time the *Rise and Shine* minibus pulled off the main Keswick to Brackenthwaite road and started the steep, narrow descent to the tiny hamlet of Lakevale.

Sitting beside Ken, the local driver who'd been hired to ferry them around for the next two weeks, Dottie marvelled at the view unfolding before her. The road twisted and turned for at least a mile and a half, passing flocks of granite-faced Herdwick sheep, a small trickle of walkers in brightly-coloured cagoules and hiking boots and a humpback bridge over a tiny stream.

The five youngsters had been chatting noisily all the way but they fell silent now. Whether they were dazed by the dramatic setting or quaking with nerves about the competition Dottie couldn't be sure.

Finally the minibus swept through a stone arch and down a rough track that bumped everyone up and down for at least half a mile.

'Ooh, I feel a bit sick,' gasped Astoria.

Dottie glanced round at her in alarm. Oh dear. Astoria did look a bit green. Mind you, it wasn't surprising she felt sick. Despite her insistence that she only ate organic food, she'd been guzzling sweets like they were going out of fashion. So too, for that matter, had the rest of them. Dottie made a mental note to limit sweets to after supper only in future.

Finally the minibus turned one last bend and drew up

outside a massive redbrick house. Stone steps led up to an incongruous-looking lime green door on which the words *Rise and Shine* had been painted in fluorescent pink. A jaunty *Rise and Shine* flag in matching colours fluttered on the roof and a banner proclaiming 'WELCOME TO THE STARSPOTTER ACADEMY' had been draped from a first-floor window.

'Over the top, or what?' Dottie murmured to Ken as they jumped out of the minibus and began dumping mounds of gear on the ground.

'A little on the jazzy side,' grinned Ken. 'This place was called Lakeview Grange last time I was here.'

Scooter, Sophy, Tommy and Kate all gathered round to help unload, taking turns to carry luggage up to the front door. The only person who didn't lift a finger was Astoria, who looked as right as rain now. She was plugged into her iPod.

'Come on Astoria,' called Sophy in her soft Scottish accent. 'We need all the help we can get here. And half this stuff seems to be yours.'

Astoria ignored her. While the others scurried up and down the steps, she calmly stood by, jiggling her head in time to her music.

Dottie felt her temper rising. The sooner Astoria was put in her place the better.

'Right, you lot,' she called to the other four. 'Do you know which cases are Astoria's?'

'That's easy,' said Kate. 'They match her outfit. Everything's red.'

'Good,' said Dottie. 'I want you to bring every bit of it back to the bus. Then we're going to let Miss Lazybones Astoria sort it out for herself. I'm sick of her letting you lot do everything for her.'

Grinning at each other, the four youngsters began dumping Astoria's baggage back in the minibus. Astoria was so engrossed in her music that she didn't notice what was going on. She only looked up when the garish front door opened and Zaza and Didi swept out.

Zaza, dressed in a giant-sized pair of denim dungarees that hung off her slight frame, a long sleeved pink T-shirt and bright yellow baseball boots, jumped down the steps and hugged each of them in turn.

'Darlings,' she squealed in excitement. 'How wonderful to see you all. We're going to have such a ball together. I can't wait. Can you?'

Didi negotiated the steps more cautiously – a sensible move considering the tight black mini skirt and high stiletto shoes she was wearing. When she got to the bottom she nodded to Dottie and uttered a curt 'hello' to the gang. She made a point of standing several yards back from them, as if she might catch something nasty if she came too close.

'We're just unloading all the cases,' said Dottie, well aware she was stating the obvious. 'Have you any idea where everyone's rooms are?'

Didi shrugged her shoulders noncommittally. She had no interest whatsoever in tiresome details such as where the finalists' rooms might be. It was bad enough being forced up here in the first place. Not only was Lakevale hundreds of miles from London, but the house looked a complete and utter dump. Thank goodness she and Zaza didn't have to stay here. Daniel had grudgingly agreed to let them check into the more luxurious Brackenside Hotel five miles up the road, where he was staying. It wasn't quite as plush as Didi would like, but it did provide room service, satellite TV, power showers and a jacuzzi.

'I think Daniel wants the crew to get some shots of the kids arriving before you take them up to their rooms,' Zaza piped up.

Dottie looked puzzled.

'Is Daniel here already then? I thought he wasn't coming till tomorrow.'

'Course he is,' said Zaza. 'Me and Didi flew up in the helicopter with him this morning. We landed in a field next to the lake. It was awesome.'

Charming, thought Dottie, livid with her boss. While she and the kids had struggled all the way to Lakevale by train and minibus – a journey that had taken all day – Daniel and the presenters had travelled in style.

'Look,' said Zaza. 'Here he is now.'

Daniel Drewsome hurried through the front door with a troubled look on his face.

'No, no, no,' he muttered, gesticulating at Dottie. 'We're not ready for you yet, kids. You'll have to jump back in the bus and drive in all over again. We need you arriving on film. We want to launch Saturday's show with the big arrival.'

Dottie's heart sank. The five youngsters were shattered after their long journey. Kate, who'd confided earlier that she'd managed to fit in her paper round as usual before dashing for the train, had huge dark circles round her eyes and Sophy looked ready to drop.

But Dottie had to concede Daniel was right. The kids' arrival would make smashing telly.

'Come on you lot,' she yelled. 'Don't worry about the luggage. Back in the minibus. Pronto.'

Zaza opened the door of the girls' dormitory with a flourish.

'Da ... daaa,' shouted the presenter, largely for the benefit of the TV crew filming the three girls' reactions from inside the room.

Kate blinked hard. The room was vast. It had freshly painted bright pink walls and floor to ceiling windows with panoramic views across Lake Valewater. Three beds,

89

each with matching pink and lime green duvets and pink drapes for privacy, had been placed along one wall. On the other side of the room stood three lime green cupboards and three dressing tables with huge heart-shaped mirrors studded with spotlights.

'D'you like it?' asked Zaza, her voice hesitant.

'Wow – it looks like something out of a fairy-tale,' gushed Kate once she was able to get her words out. 'Oh Zaza, thank you. I've never seen such a pretty room. I can't believe it's for us. Thank you so so much.'

Sophy's expression was a mirror image of Kate's. The tall Scottish girl darted across the room, performed a delighted twirl and then threw herself full-length on the bed nearest to the window.

'That's a yes, I take it?' laughed Zaza.

Sophy's shining eyes said everything.

'I love it,' she shrieked, then rushed to give Zaza a hug.

Next Zaza turned to Astoria, who was still standing in the doorway.

'I thought we'd at least have our own rooms,' said Astoria coolly. 'I'm not used to sharing. I need my own space. That's what I've got at home.'

Kate could scarcely believe her ears. What a horrible girl Astoria was. In an instant her excitement evaporated – like a balloon being popped. Somehow Astoria's scorn had taken all the fun away and Kate felt desperately homesick. She longed for her mum.

Sophy and Zaza both looked as shocked as she did. Sophy sat motionless on her bed, open-mouthed at Astoria's rudeness, while Zaza, lost for words, shifted awkwardly from one foot to the other. This was the last reaction she'd expected.

The crew, however, reacted with their feet. Without uttering a single word to each other, they stopped filming instantly and began shifting their gear out of the room.

'Spoilt brat,' muttered the man with the sound boom as he squeezed past Astoria.

'Big mistake,' mumbled the cameraman under his breath. 'We don't like toffee-nosed brats.'

'I'm not toffee-nosed,' protested Astoria indignantly. 'I didn't mean it. If you let me give my answer again I'll say whatever you want…'

But it was too late. The crew, with Zaza in hot pursuit, had gone.

The three girls, shocked by what had happened, stared at one another.

Kate was the first to break the silence.

'You really shouldn't have said that, Astoria,' she whispered. '*Rise and Shine* have done their best for us. And Dottie and Zaza have been so kind. It was so, so … ungrateful.'

'And now look what's happened,' retorted Sophy, joining in. 'Everyone was being really nice to us, really welcoming. And now they've gone and marched off in a huff. And it's all your fault.'

Astoria, at twelve the youngest of the three girls, looked dumbfounded by Kate and Sophy's onslaught. She wasn't used to people turning on her like this. At home her mum and dad hung on her every word and while she wasn't exactly the most popular girl in the class at Kidstars, she at least commanded a grudging sort of respect.

'Well it's true,' persisted Astoria. 'I did think we'd get our own rooms. Didn't you…?'

Kate shrugged her shoulders. If she was honest she was glad to be sharing with the other girls. She'd been dreading being left on her own.

'Hang on a minute,' said Sophy slowly. 'I've got an idea …'

Astoria's eyes narrowed with suspicion.

'What?'

'Why don't we ask Dottie if you can have your own private room? Then me and Kate can share this one and you can be by yourself. Just like you wanted.'

Kate agreed to Sophy's plan with alacrity.

'That's brilliant,' she said. 'Come on. Let's go and find Dottie. She'll sort it. I know she will.'

Astoria followed Kate and Sophy down the stairs, cursing herself inwardly. Why had she made such a stupid fuss about the room? All she'd succeeded in doing was putting everyone's backs up and bonding Kate and Sophy together. If she didn't watch out, she was going to be completely left in the cold.

Astoria Lennox was far too self-centred to see it but she was her own worst enemy. If she'd only swallowed her pride right there and then and admitted to the other girls that she'd been an idiot and would far rather share with them, they would have welcomed her with open arms. But as it was, half an hour later an exasperated Dottie was showing her into a tiny box room on the top floor. The window was so high up Astoria couldn't see out of it and there was only space for a iron bedstead, a chest of drawers and a wonky-looking hat stand to hang her clothes on.

'This is nice and tucked out of the way, isn't it,' said Dottie cheerily. 'Rather you than me, Astoria, but no one will disturb you up here. It's all yours …'

12
GG's Dance Class

TAP TAP tap. Tap tap tap.

Astoria awoke with a start. What *was* that noise? What was her mum knocking on her bedroom door for? She usually whizzed straight in with tea and toast on a tray and a cheery 'Morning darling.'

Slowly Astoria's sleep-befuddled brain cleared. Oh no. She wasn't in her warm, cosy bed in Streatham at all. She was in a freezing-cold, spooky attic bedroom at the Starspotter Academy.

Her heart beating frantically, Astoria shivered and wrapped the duvet tighter around her. She'd only been away for a day and yet already she was missing her home comforts more than she would ever have dreamed possible. A wave of misery swept over her. She'd never felt so wretched in her entire life.

How could she have been so pig-headed about the dormitory downstairs? Why couldn't she have kept her silly mouth shut? It hadn't been *that* bad. All things considered, it had been cosy and welcoming – what with its old-fashioned radiators, extra blankets piled high on the beds and thick drapes, padded for extra warmth. *And* she'd have had the other girls to chat to.

This room couldn't be more different. Not only was it titchy, but the wooden floor boards creaked, and even though it was the middle of July, the windows had rattled all night in the wind. If Kate and Sophy had been up here too it might have been funny pretending there were ghosts wafting around. But, all by herself, Astoria had been terrified out of her wits.

'Who is it?' she called out. Her voice sounded strangely feeble – not at all like her usual confident one.

'It's us,' Sophy called back in her distinctive Scottish burr. 'Me and Kate, I mean. It's eight o'clock. We've come to get you for breakfast. We're both ravenous and Dottie says our first dance class starts at eight thirty. You'd better get your skates on.'

Astoria jumped out of bed and padded across the creaky floor in bare feet. Sophy and Kate must have been leaning against the door because when she opened it they practically fell into the room. Astoria glanced at them, making a quick mental note of their outfits. She didn't want to be outdone. Not on the first day – no way. But in fact both girls were dressed casually, in tracksuit bottoms, T-shirts and trainers. Sophy's trainers were bright pink, with scarlet go-faster stripes. Kate's had frayed laces and were falling to bits.

Kate didn't notice Astoria looking her up and down. She was too busy staring at Astoria's new room, taking in the shabby metal bedstead and peeling rose-sprigged wallpaper. She couldn't believe her eyes. The dormitory downstairs was like a palace compared to this. It was almost as damp as Bright Street up here – and that was saying something.

'Oh,' she said, trying – and failing – to mask her surprise. 'This isn't at all what I was expecting,' she said.

'Me neither,' agreed Sophy, visibly shocked. Then, seeing Astoria's face crumple, she added: 'But it's very nice. And really, really quiet. We're right above the kitchen and the cooks have been clattering about for hours. But you'll be able to get away from everything up here, won't you?'

Astoria wasn't sure she *wanted* to get away from

everything any more. Clattering or no clattering, she'd give anything to be in the dormitory downstairs with Kate and Sophy. But she couldn't bear the thought of the two girls feeling sorry for her so she tried to put a brave face on things.

'I will, won't I?' she said briskly. 'Now, I'm not being funny, but could you leave me to get dressed by myself? I'll meet you downstairs in a couple of minutes.'

Dottie had treated them all to fish and chips in the kitchen the night before so this was the first time the Starspotter gang had ventured into the dining hall.

The room was long and narrow, with a stuffed deer's head above the door and portraits of po-faced previous inhabitants lining the wood-panelled walls. The *Rise and Shine* team had done their best to liven the surroundings up a bit by kitting it out with a bright pink dining table, lime green chairs and a chrome juke box in the corner.

'Wicked,' shrieked Sophy when she spotted the juke box. 'Let's put something really groovy on.'

She pressed a few buttons at random and instantly Eminem's latest hit blasted out, shattering the peace and quiet.

'They'll be able to hear that the other side of the lake,' chuckled Tommy.

'Come on, let's turn it up a bit higher then,' sniggered Scooter.

The deafening racket brought Dottie rushing into the room within seconds.

'Ssssh,' she hissed, quickly turning the volume down. 'Ssssssssssssssh. What are you lot like? You'll wake Daniel at his hotel halfway up the valley at this rate. And the last thing I need right now is Daniel sticking his blooming oar in everything at this unearthly hour. I have to put up with enough aggro from him as it is.'

'Oh no,' whinged Scooter in mock protest. 'I can hardly hear it now.'

'Well, you've obviously got a problem with your hearing,' retorted Dottie briskly, refusing to put up with any nonsense. 'I'd better book you an appointment with the doctor. Now you lot, it's going to be a really demanding day today. There's a two-hour dance class with GG in the ballroom for starters…'

'Who's GG?' interrupted Scooter with a guffaw of laughter. 'Sounds more like a horse than a dance teacher.'

Dottie stared at him coldly.

'GG is the toughest dance instructor in the business,' she told him. 'You'll be laughing the other side of your face after a couple of hours with her. And after that, you've got voice training, music appreciation and an assertiveness training session.'

'I can think of one person around here who certainly doesn't need any assertiveness training,' muttered Tommy to Scooter.

'Hang on a minute,' said Dottie, suddenly noticing that there were only four of them. 'Where has Astoria got to?'

'She's on her way,' said Kate quickly. 'We woke her up at eight and she said she'd be down as fast as she could.'

'Phew – that's a relief,' said Dottie. 'I thought we'd lost her for a minute.'

'I wish,' whispered Tommy.

'Right,' continued Dottie, choosing to ignore Tommy's jibe. 'As I've said, it's going to be hectic, so you must all eat a hearty breakfast. I know I probably sound like all your mums rolled into one but you'll need lots of fuel to keep you going. Oh, and here is a list of the rules of the Starspotter Academy. Take a deco at these and I'll pop my head round the door later.'

Dottie handed everyone a lime green sheet of paper.

Scooter took one look at his and grimaced in disgust.

'Ugh,' he grumbled. 'It's just like being back at primary school.'

The others glanced at their copies with interest.

Starspotter Academy: House Rules

Remember to be kind, helpful and considerate to your fellow competitors

Listen to what the *Rise and Shine* teachers and presenters say

Work hard

Arrive for lessons and meals on time

Starspotter will be demanding – make sure you get plenty of sleep

Unless there is an emergency, contact with family and friends is banned

Mobile phones are strictly forbidden

Enjoy the next ten days!

Kate, Sophy, Tommy and Scooter obeyed Dottie to the letter, tucking into cereal, toast, eggs and bacon, washed down by freshly squeezed orange juice and cups of steaming hot tea.

'Mmm – that was fab,' said Scooter when he'd finished. He pushed his plate away and rubbed his tummy appreciatively. 'Just what I needed. Go to work on a good breakfast – that's what my dad always says.'

Kate hadn't eaten a breakfast like it in years. Back home in Gribblesdale it was very different. Her mum made porridge for her most mornings before she left for the factory but Kate rarely ate it, preferring to buy a chocolate bar and a can of Coke at the newsagent's once she'd finished her paper round.

'I feel a million times better,' she said. 'I can't think when I last had so much energy. I could climb to the top of a mountain and still have loads left over.'

'That's what I like to hear,' said Daniel Drewsome, appearing unexpectedly in the doorway. He was wearing his customary white T-shirt and black leather trousers and looked as if he hadn't shaved for days.

'Now come on, you horrible lot, I want you in the ballroom straightaway. And don't go all camera-shy on me because the crew are going to be filming you on and off throughout the day. We're doing an item for tomorrow's *Rise and Shine* on your first day at the Starspotter Academy. So make sure you're on tip-top form. Any slackers will be on the first train out of here. Understand?'

'Stretch those arms. Stretch as high as you can. Come on, Scooter, you're not trying. Give it more *oomph*. That's good, Kate. Keep going. You're doing well.'

A stream of sweat trickled down Kate's brow. She dashed it away impatiently. She'd thought she was fit, what with all that cycling and two nights a week soccer training at school. But she'd never worked so hard in her entire life. Dottie clearly hadn't been joking when she'd warned the group that Grace Graves, Starspotter's resident dance teacher, would work them into the ground.

GG, as she was always known, was far steelier than she looked. She was tiny, with dark hair cut short in an elfin bob and arms that looked as though they might snap if they did anything too arduous. That was a laugh thought Kate as she struggled to keep up. GG was stronger than the rest of them put together.

The dance instructor's make-up was extraordinary too – lips painted scarlet and a deathly white powdered face. She wore a black leotard with matching leggings and red ballet shoes that laced up her slender calves.

Dottie had already told them about GG's dazzling career, first as part of a famous dance troupe in the West End and more recently as a stage choreographer.

'She's worked with all the top names,' Dottie had said, 'so you'd better work blooming hard for her or she'll go ballistic. And be warned. She may look like sweetness and light but I wouldn't like to be on the sharp side of her tongue, I can tell you. The words "tough" and "old boots" come to mind.'

Kate glanced at the old-fashioned clock on the ballroom wall. It had just gone nine so they'd been going for exactly half an hour. A worried expression flickered across her brow. Where could Astoria have got to? Why hadn't she appeared yet? GG seemed to have completely forgotten about her.

Without thinking, Kate put her hand up.

'Excuse me, miss,' she said tentatively.

'GG,' snapped the dance teacher. 'Call me GG. Everyone does. Now what's the matter, Kate? Are you flagging already? Honestly…kids these days. No stamina whatsoever. I don't know what the world's coming to.'

Kate bit her lip. She didn't want to draw attention to Astoria's absence. Or land her in hot water. But she felt really anxious about her.

'It's Astoria, miss,' said Kate, then corrected herself. 'Er, I mean GG.'

'Who's Astoria?' snapped GG, her voice impatient. 'What a ridiculous name.'

'The other Starspotter girl,' said Sophy, trying to help Kate out.

'Oh her,' said GG dismissively. 'What about her?'

'She hasn't come down yet. So I wondered …'

'Wondered what?'

'If I ought to go and find her. She might have got lost.'

'Hrrrmmpphh,' barked GG. 'The academy is not *that* big. She must have a very poor sense of direction if she's lost her way.'

It wasn't much of a joke but Scooter and Tommy hooted with laughter all the same.

GG fixed them both with a cool stare, then sucked in her breath disapprovingly.

'From what I have seen of your group so far,' she said, 'I am far from impressed. It's clear that I must set ground rules for this class. Honestly, youngsters today. I can see that discipline is sadly lacking in all your lives. And if you don't have discipline, you will get precisely nowhere in your careers. Do I make myself clear?'

'What's discipline, miss?' asked Scooter. Despite his innocent-looking demeanour, Scooter was rapidly emerging as the Starspotter joker.

GG glared at him.

'Have any of you got the faintest idea what it takes to succeed in this business?' she demanded.

None of them said anything. Sophy bit her lip and looked embarrassed, while Kate stared fixedly at the parquet floor. She didn't want to risk igniting GG's temper any further by catching her eye.

'That's presuming you want to succeed,' added GG. 'Maybe you don't. Although if that is the case I can't think what you're doing here in the first place. It's not a holiday camp you know.'

Again they all remained silent. The crew had stopped filming during GG's tirade and dumped their equipment on the floor. Daniel Drewsome had asked for electrifying shots of the finalists' amazing dance talents, not a rant. Even Scooter had realised this was not the time to be cracking jokes and shut up.

'To succeed in this business,' GG continued, 'you need three things. Does anyone know what they are?'

'Blood, sweat and tears,' murmured Sophy, who'd often heard the phrase from her dad.

GG paced round the class, glaring at each of the

youngsters in turn. She looked, thought Kate, like a tiger ready to pounce.

'What was that, Sophy?' she demanded.

'Er, blood, sweat and tears?'

'Good girl,' said GG approvingly. 'At least *someone* has got the right idea. I was really beginning to wonder. Yes, first of all you need *talent*. Now you've all got that – you wouldn't be here otherwise – but talent is the tip of the iceberg. You need much much more than that. The second thing you need is *self-belief*. You must believe in yourselves, have the will to succeed. If you don't have self-belief then you may as well pack your bags and go home now. Do I make myself understood?'

The group murmured their assent. Even Scooter was paying attention now.

'And the third thing you need,' said GG. 'The most important thing of all is …'

Suddenly the double doors of the ballroom shot open and Astoria raced in at high speed. GG was so startled that she stopped what she was saying in mid-flow.

The rest of the Starspotter group gaped open-mouthed at their fellow contestant. Firstly, at the horrifying prospect of GG going up the wall again. And secondly, because Astoria looked even more extraordinary than usual.

'Wow,' mumbled Kate, wide-eyed with admiration. She glanced down in disgust at her shabby joggers. She'd give anything for an outfit like that.

'What *does* she think she looks like?' whispered Scooter to Tommy.

'Dunno,' said Tommy, pole-axed. 'A bit um … purple, I s'ppose.'

While the rest of them were clad in tracksuit pants and T-shirts or vests, Astoria had dressed up to the nines. She wore skin-tight lilac trousers, cropped to the knee, a matching vest with her name picked out in silver and purple ballet pumps. When Kate and Sophy had seen her earlier her blonde hair had been wild and unkempt, but now it was sleek and gorgeous, hanging down her back like silk.

GG didn't bat an eyelid at Astoria's appearance.

'And the third thing you need to succeed in this business is… what?' she asked, looking keenly at Astoria.

Kate gulped nervously. Astoria wouldn't have a clue what the dance teacher was on about. Mind you, she couldn't help because she didn't know the answer either.

'Hard work,' piped up Astoria smugly.

The rest of the class did a double take at this. Tommy and Scooter had been winking at each other, relishing the delicious anticipation of Astoria Lennox making a complete and utter fool of herself.

'How did she work that one out?' mouthed Sophy in Kate's direction.

Kate gave a half-shrug, not daring to risk GG's wrath by speaking.

If GG was surprised, she didn't show it.

'Good,' she declared smoothly. 'Very good. So remember, the rest of you, talent and self-belief are important but you won't get anywhere if you don't work hard too. Talent, self-belief and hard work – that's what it takes. Now let's get back to it.'

'*Jammy beggar*,' muttered Scooter, livid that Astoria had escaped the telling-off he'd expected. How she got away with things he had no idea.

The rest of the class flew by. GG put them through their routines over and over again till they were absolutely perfect. Ten minutes before the end of the lesson she signalled to the crew to start filming again, confident that the group's performance was as good as she could expect on the first day.

'Your mums and dads will be dead impressed when they watch this on the show tomorrow,' she told the youngsters. 'Well done, everyone, it took a while - but you've pulled it off. I'll see you back here at eight-thirty on Sunday for more of the same.'

'Don't we get a lie-in on Sunday?' scowled Astoria.

'No you do not. Oh, and by the way, Astoria, I would like to see you in my office in five minutes time. It's next to the drawing room and my name is on the door. Can you manage that all right? You won't get lost this time, will you?'

'I should think so too,' whispered Tommy. 'Little Miss Stuck-Up Prima Donna. Serves her right if GG lets rip. It's about time someone took her down a peg or two.'

13
Daniel's Dressing-Down

KATE WAS worn out by the end of the first day. She'd always assumed she had loads of stamina, but after GG's dance class, a voice training session with a coach called Misty Blue, assertiveness training with Daniel Drewsome and yet another singing lesson, she wasn't so sure. All she craved now were a shower, a mug of hot chocolate and then bed.

If anything, Daniel's lesson had been even more scary than GG's. Dottie was forever taking the mickey out of Daniel and calling him jokey names, but Kate thought he was utterly terrifying. She'd been frightened out of her wits when he'd bellowed at her to speak up at that first audition in Manchester and nothing had changed now.

He'd begun the assertiveness session by instructing the five finalists to take bright pink wooden chairs from the side of the ballroom and arrange them in a circle. Then he'd asked each of them in turn to describe on camera the best things about themselves – not counting singing, dancing, acting or composing.

Sophy kicked off by saying she was a loyal friend, had a wicked sense of humour and could juggle six balls in the air at once.

Scooter, confident as ever, claimed he was kind, charming and sensationally good-looking.

'And that's not all,' he beamed. 'I'm ace at drawing racing cars and I can hop on one leg and rub my tummy at the same time.'

'Now that'll come in very handy, I'm sure,' said Daniel dryly.

Tommy told the *Rise and Shine* director that he'd been Grove Park Wanderers' leading goal scorer last season.

Astoria, who'd been a little subdued at the start of the session following her ferocious dressing-down from GG, relished the chance to talk about her talents. She declared she was the most popular girl at Kidstars, had raised £1,405.56p for the NSPCC last year and always gave her pocket money to 'children less fortunate than myself.'

'Ugh – pass the sick bag, Astoria,' grunted Scooter. Then, realising the camera was still rolling, he clapped his hand over his mouth in mock horror.

'That's very touching, Astoria,' said Daniel. No one was sure whether he was being sarcastic or felt genuinely moved by Astoria's boasting. 'And you, Kate? What are your best qualities?'

Kate had opened her mouth to say something – only nothing came out. The seconds ticked by. She tried again but nothing happened. Her throat felt oddly dry, strangulated by nerves.

'Come on, Kate,' said Daniel, getting less patient by the second. 'We haven't got all day.'

Kate stared out of the ballroom window, mesmerised by the breathtaking view across Lake Valewater. The water glistened in the late afternoon sun. A steamer packed with tourists chugged past, while in the distance dozens of tiny dinghies tacked back and forth, sails flapping in the wind. She could just about make out a couple of tiny matchstick figures in bright orange life jackets on board each one.

'*KATE!*' roared Daniel yet again, making her jump in alarm. '*Will you please pay attention? Your best quality. Now. We haven't got all day.*'

'Er, er sorry,' muttered Kate, still tongue-tied. Quality, quality, quality, she thought, frantically racking her brain for inspiration. 'Er. I'm the best paper girl in Gribblesdale. I cook a mean bacon sandwich. And I love my mum.'

'This gets more excruciating by the second,' groaned Scooter, putting his head in his hands. '*Aaah… Katie loves her mum.* Yuk. I want to throw up on the spot.'

'Good girl,' Daniel said gruffly. 'Just a little on the slow side. You got there in the end but make sure you sharpen up your act next time, OK?'

'OK,' said Kate meekly. Inside she was mortified. The others had all been so slick, so quick to reel off their answers. How could she ever compete with them? They were brilliant.

'Now the reason I asked you to describe your best characteristics was to boost your confidence,' continued Daniel. 'For goodness sake, if you don't think you're wonderfully fab in every way then how are you going to convince the viewers? Lesson number one: You've got to believe in yourself.'

'That's not a problem a certain person has,' whispered Scooter, stealing a sly glance at Astoria. 'She thinks *wonderfully fab* is a complete understatement of her talents.'

The working day finished up with a 30-minute singing tutorial, led by a man called Garcia Andrew. The name didn't mean anything whatsoever to Scooter, Tommy, Sophy or Astoria, who all pulled blank faces when Dottie mentioned his name. Kate, however, beamed with pleasure. Garcia Andrew was her mum's favourite singer. He'd had a couple of minor hits five or six years back, *Your Face* and *Time to Part*, then disappeared without trace. But Linda Barnsley had never forgotten him. She adored his deep soulful voice and played his album almost every night on the battered old CD player in the kitchen at Bright Street.

'Wow,' said Kate when it was her turn to be introduced. 'My mum loves your records.'

'She's clearly a woman of exquisite taste, your mum,' chuckled Garcia. He was more than six feet tall, with curly brown hair and twinkly brown eyes. He wore a double-breasted suit made of aubergine velvet, a stripy pink scarf and black patent winkle-picker shoes.

'Yes she is,' beamed Kate. 'I, I… don't suppose you'd give me your autograph, would you? It's her birthday tomorrow and she'd be made up with it.'

Daniel was watching this exchange, but before Garcia could reply he interjected sharply.

'Come on Garcia, get it moving, will you? This is not the Garcia Andrew fan club, Kate. Now, I need a couple more minutes filming for tomorrow's show and then it's a wrap.'

'Sure,' drawled Garcia. 'Right you lot, this afternoon we're going to learn to sing *a capella*. Does anyone know what *a capella* is?'

'It means unaccompanied,' piped up Astoria. 'We do it all the time at Kidstars.'

'Do you now?' said Garcia. 'You're Astoria, right?'

'Yes,' said Astoria self-importantly.

'Well seeing as you sing *a capella* all the time, I'd like you to sit this one out. As for the rest of you, here are the words I want you to sing.'

Garcia handed everyone except Astoria a printed sheet. Astoria looked thunderous. How dare he leave her out? And when the cameras were filming too. It wasn't fair.

'Right,' said Garcia. 'I'll sing each line first and then I want you to follow.'

Dottie had tears in her eyes when she wandered into the ballroom to hear the finished result. The purity of the youngsters' voices, unencumbered by any instruments or backing track was wonderful to hear. Maybe she was going soft in the head but it was worth enduring all Daniel's paltry demands to be standing here listening to this.

At the end of the session, Garcia thanked the youngsters for their hard work and told them they'd do it all over again the following day. Astoria was so livid at being excluded that she stalked out of the ballroom the instant he'd finished.

Kate toyed with the idea of asking Garcia for his autograph again but it was too late. Daniel had collared him and the two men were deep in conversation. She'd just picked up her tracksuit top and was heading for the door when Daniel called her name.

Kate's heart sank. Please don't let Daniel have another go at me, she prayed. Especially not in front of Garcia. She'd die of embarrassment if he did.

'Kate, can you come over here? Quick as you can, sweetheart. Garcia's got an idea.'

14
Linda's Stupendous Surprise

LINDA BARNSLEY curled up on the tatty red armchair in Bright Street. A mug of tea and a plate of buttered toast lay untouched beside her. She was far too nervous to eat. She could barely think straight, let alone do anything else.

The TV weathermen had been predicting a heatwave for days now but there was no sign of it in Gribblesdale. The sky was grey and overcast – mirroring Linda's mood.

Kate had only been away for a couple of days but it felt like forever. To make things worse it was Wakes Week at Brydale's, the textile factory where Linda worked. Most factories in the area shut up shop for a week every summer to allow all their staff a holiday. Each town had its favourite holiday spot for Wakes Week and Gribblesdale's was Blackpool. Most of Linda's friends were there now, riding the dodgems and paddling in the sea. But Linda was stony broke and couldn't afford to go. Anyhow, it wouldn't be the same without Kate.

Linda had barely got a wink of sleep all night. She had been counting the minutes till nine on Saturday morning. All contact between the Starspotter finalists and their families had been banned – Daniel Drewsome claimed it would be far too disruptive for everyone. So Linda had no idea how Kate was getting on. She couldn't wait to see her on *Rise and Shine*.

109

At nine on the dot the jaunty *Rise and Shine* theme tune blasted out of Linda's dodgy telly. An old wire coat hanger had to make do as an aerial and every now and again the Barnsleys had to bang the top of the TV to make it work. The colour was a bit hit and miss too, so when Zaza and Didi burst on to the screen they looked even more crazy than usual. Zaza's hair was in bright pink bunches while Didi's was a peculiar shade of emerald green. They wore matching fluorescent yellow outfits and appeared to be standing by a purple lake, with lilac sailing boats bobbing about behind them.

'We've got a very special show for you this week,' grinned Zaza, twirling one of her bunches round with her finger.

'We most certainly have,' butted in Didi. She'd not only stolen Zaza's lines but proceeded to elbow her out of the way while she was at it. 'It's the first week of our amazing Starspotter final. We've got five incredible contestants and they are all going to sing live for you.'

'I bet you're wondering where we are,' said Zaza, attempting to sound conspiratorial.

'Not much point asking you,' said Didi spitefully. 'You can't even find your way to the hotel dining room.'

Judging by the furious look on Zaza's face, it was clear that that last remark hadn't been in the script. Didi was ad-libbing for dear life now.

'Honestly, some people …' began Zaza. Then she stopped, wisely deciding not to rise to Didi's bait. 'Actually we're at a top secret location in the Lake District. And isn't it fab? We've got breathtaking countryside, lovely people and five sensational young singers. Life really couldn't get much better.'

'Over the next week we're going to get to know our five superstars very well,' said Didi. 'They'll be performing live for us today. And then …'

'And then,' said Zaza, smoothly nicking Didi's lines. Two could play at that game. 'And then, next Saturday, a week from today, you'll have the chance to vote for your favourite young star.'

'Speed it up, girls,' said a voice in the girls' earpieces. 'We need to go to the pre-recorded stuff now. Come on, *pronto.*'

The sound of Daniel Drewsome's gravelly drawl made both of them jump. As usual Didi recovered her composure first.

'Right,' she said. 'Let's meet our five amazing finalists. And number one is … Scooter Mason from Slough in Berkshire. Come on, give it up for Scooter.'

At home in Gribblesdale, Linda Barnsley sat bolt upright. Her back was rigid and her fists were clenched. She was longing for her first glimpse of Kate.

A couple of pretty Lakeland scenes appeared on the screen, followed by a shot of an express train arriving at Penrith station. Then, just as Linda thought she was going to explode with impatience … there was Kate. And best of all, she looked her usual self – a little shy perhaps, but happy and smiling.

Linda leaned forward to get a closer look at her daughter and sighed with pleasure. The first shot of Kate, standing on the station platform with the other finalists, was followed by an image of her unloading piles of luggage outside the Starspotter Academy. After that came Kate in a dance class, doubled up with laughter at a joke cracked by one of the other finalists, and Kate tucking into a hearty plate of fish and chips.

Linda wiped a tear from her eye. Her emotions were completely up the creek today. One moment she felt a fierce sense of pride that Kate was on national telly. The next she yearned for her daughter to walk into the sitting room and slump down on the sofa next to her.

111

The next twenty minutes of the programme passed in a blur as one by one the other contestants introduced themselves and each got the chance to perform live. By the time she'd watched Scooter, Astoria, Sophy and Tommy zip through their paces, Linda reckoned she'd got the measure of all of them. Scooter was the cheeky one, forever cracking jokes. Astoria was full of herself but undoubtedly had talent. Sophy was gorgeous-looking – and sweet-natured too. Tommy danced like an angel but wasn't as noisy as Scooter. They were a talented bunch. How would her Kate compare?

Waiting in the ballroom for her turn to sing, Kate felt her tummy turn over with nerves. Dottie squeezed her hand reassuringly. As *Rise and Shine*'s assistant producer cum dogsbody she'd been fussing over the finalists like a mother hen all morning. First she'd insisted they all eat a good breakfast at seven-thirty. She'd made them all do a thirty-minute warm-up with GG, then ushered them into a short voice class with Garcia.

'There's nothing to worry about,' Dottie kept on telling them. 'Just do exactly the same as you did yesterday and everything will be fine.'

'That's easy for you to say,' whinged Tommy. 'How are we supposed to forget that there are millions of people watching us?'

'Can you see them?' demanded Dottie.

'Well no, not exactly,' admitted Tommy.

'D'you know what they look like?'

'Course not,' said Tommy.

'So don't think about them,' said Dottie. 'Problem solved.'

Kate tried to obliterate the audience watching at home from her mind. If only Tommy hadn't brought the subject up. The only way she could focus on the task ahead was to pretend she was performing for the people in the ballroom – namely Dottie, Garcia, GG, Sophy, Scooter, Tommy, Astoria and the four-piece band behind them.

'… And now it's time for our fifth fantabulous finalist,' roared Zaza. 'She's thirteen-years-old, she's from Gribblesdale in Lancashire, and that big voice of hers will knock your socks off. Put your hands together for Kate Barnsley.'

As Kate stepped forward, Linda Barnsley's heart began beating even faster than before. Kate looked gorgeous, she thought. Her long dark hair, usually drawn back in a scruffy pony tail for school, had been brushed till it shone and she was wearing it loose and flowing. Linda had dreaded the *Rise and Shine* team turning her daughter into something she wasn't. Kate was such a tomboy – she wouldn't look right all glammed up to the nines. But in fact she was wearing pink velvet flares and a short-sleeved navy T-shirt with her name picked out in pink sequins, exactly the sort of outfit she'd choose for herself.

Kate opened her mouth to sing and instinctively Linda crossed her fingers so tight they hurt. Kate launched into the haunting opening bars of the Beatles classic, *Yesterday*, building line by line to show the amazing power of her voice.

'Oh love,' whispered Linda as the number drew to a close and Kate took a hesitant bow. 'Oh love. I'm that proud of you.'

But that wasn't the end of it. As the music died away, Zaza and Didi sashayed to Kate's side once more. Zaza gave her a huge hug and the ever-aloof Didi shook her hand.

'That was fantastic, Kate,' said Zaza. 'It really was. Now tell me, haven't you got something special you want to share with the viewers at home?'

'Er, yes,' said Kate. She wished she could sound as witty and natural as Sophy and the others, but for the second day running her mind had turned to mush. All she could feel was relief that she'd got to the end of the song without drying up or getting lost in the tricky middle chorus.

'Come on then,' prompted Didi sharply. 'Spill the beans.'

Once again, Kate hesitated. They'd rehearsed this a million times yesterday but she still couldn't get the words out.

'You've got a surprise for someone special, *haven't you*?' said Didi. A trace of impatience was clearly discernible in her tone.

'Yes,' said Kate. Even with the hidden microphone amplifying every sound, her voice was barely audible.

Didi rolled her eyes. This girl might have a powerful voice once she got going, but she didn't stand a hope in hell of turning into a pop star. She was making a right pig's ear of this interview.

All of a sudden Kate felt a comforting arm creep around her shoulders and Zaza took over the conversation.

'You're doing fine, Kate,' murmured Zaza under her breath. 'Just keep going. Don't lose your nerve now.'

Watching at home, Linda saw Kate visibly relax. It was clear that Zaza was a million times easier to talk to than her co-presenter. Didi seemed totally oblivious to the fact that Kate was only thirteen and not used to being on telly. What did she expect? For goodness sake, Kate had barely been out of Gribblesdale till a few months ago.

'Today's a special day for your mum, isn't it, Kate?' said Zaza. 'Can you tell us about it?'

'It's my mum's birthday,' Kate began. Comforted by Zaza's intervention, a more confident note had crept into her voice. A few seconds before, her eyes had darted all over the place, but now she stared straight at the camera. 'She's called Linda Barnsley and she's the best mum in the whole wide world. It's just me and her at home and she

114

works so hard to give me everything. So I wanted to say "Happy Birthday" and tell her that I love her. Oh, and I've hidden a special present for her under the settee in our front room.'

The tears were streaming down Linda's face by this time. With Kate away in the Lakes, she hadn't given her birthday a second thought. She should have known that Kate would organise something. It was typical of her.

'And you've got an extra special treat in store for your mum, haven't you?' said Zaza. 'Can you tell us about it?'

'My mum's favourite singer of all time is Garcia Andrew,' said Kate, her face lighting up as she chatted to Zaza. 'It's such a coincidence because when we arrived at the Starspotter Academy I discovered that Garcia is our singing tutor. And when I told him how my mum's always going on about him and that she's thirty-five today, he came up with this idea that we should sing a duet together. For my mum, I mean…'

Sick of being sidelined by Zaza, Didi moved into shot again.

'So now,' she bellowed, 'singing the golden oldie hit *Your Face*, are Garcia Andrew and Kate Barnsley.'

When Linda ventured out of the house later that morning, Mrs Tate, the elderly next-door neighbour who'd always had a soft spot for Kate, was waiting for her.

'Your Kate did you right proud this morning,' she said.

'She did, didn't she?' beamed Linda.

'It's not my type of cup of tea, pet, that sort of music – I prefer a bit of Frank Sinatra myself. But do you know what?'

'What?' asked Linda.

'That lass of yours. She reminds me of Gracie Fields. She's going to win, you know. You mark my words.'

And so it went on. Everywhere she went – the supermarket, the newsagent's, the chippy – people tapped Linda on the shoulder and congratulated her on Kate's performance. Even grumpy old Mr Raven, one of the people Kate delivered papers to, waylaid her in the street.

'She wasn't half bad, your girl,' he said gruffly. 'But tell her to get back on that paper round. The lad who came this morning brought me the bloomin' *Despatch*. Youngsters these days. They've got no idea. What do I want with the *Despatch*?'

Hearing this, Linda beamed with pride for the umpteenth time. Coming from Mr Raven, this was a compliment of the highest order. She must remember to tell Kate.

By the time Linda got back to Bright Street two hours later, she was startled to find a young man in a sharply-cut charcoal suit hovering on the doorstep. She'd never set eyes on him before. He looked completely out of place in a factory town like Gribblesdale for a start. No one ever wore a suit unless they were going to a wedding. Or a funeral. And not always then. Not only that, but he was carrying a shiny black briefcase.

The young man smiled broadly at Linda.

'Mrs Barnsley?' he asked.

A shiver of alarm ran down Linda's spine. She was behind with the payments on a couple of clothes catalogues. But sending someone out to collect the money on a Saturday was odd. And anyway, after buying a loaf of bread, carton of milk, this week's *Bella* magazine and a portion of chips, she was right out of cash. There was no way she could pay him.

Linda dumped her shopping on the ground and began rifling in her pocket for her front door key.

'Who wants to know?'

The young man laughed and flashed a card in front of her face.

Emblazoned across it in fancy silver lettering were the words *Dean Barry, Reporter, North Star News Agency.*

'That's me,' said the young man jauntily. 'We saw *Rise and Shine* in the office this morning and we'd like to do a story about you and your daughter.'

Linda's face looked a picture.

'What?' she spluttered. 'But why?'

'You're both celebrities now, love. The whole world saw Katie sing that song for you this morning.'

'Kate,' corrected Linda.

'Sorry, Kate. But this is the kind of story that goes down a treat with the papers. It's got everything – a pretty girl, a birthday, telly, the real "ah" factor.'

Linda wasn't sure what the 'ah' factor was when it was at home. In fact she couldn't understand a word of what Dean Barry was on about.

'So what does it involve?' she asked.

'Simple,' said Dean, quick as a flash. 'A little chat. Oh, and a picture of you.'

Without waiting for an answer, Dean beckoned to a man sitting in a silver saloon parked on the other side of Bright Street.

'Over here, mate,' he shouted.

A balding, middle-aged man in a blue shirt and beige trousers that were too tight for him got out of the car and ambled across the street. He had a camera slung round his neck and a large bag over one shoulder. Linda took one look at him and panicked. She was wearing a pair of Kate's cast off jeans and a crumpled pink T-shirt she'd found at the bottom of the ironing basket. She hadn't even brushed her hair this morning.

'Don't be daft,' Linda told Dean hurriedly. 'I look a right dog's breakfast. I can't possibly have my picture

117

taken now. Come back on Monday and I'll think about it.'

'You look fine, love,' said Dean. 'Doesn't she, Gary?'

Gary Parkes, the photographer, was blessed with a little more panache than his reporter colleague.

'Hi Linda,' he said. 'I'm Gary Parkes, the picture man. Your Kate was a real credit to you this morning. What a lovely girl she is. So natural and unspoilt. My kids aren't a patch on her. Glued to the *PlayStation* 24/7 they are.'

This was the way to Linda's heart.

'Thank you. But can't you do all this another day? I could get my hair done or something.'

'You look absolutely stunning as you are,' said Gary, laying on the charm with a trowel. 'It's easy to see where Kate gets her looks from. Now Linda, I tell you what. You go and put a nice bit of lippy on and you'll look just perfect.'

Before she knew it, Linda was leading Gary and Dean into number 14 and settling them in the front room.

'All right, just give me a couple of minutes to do my face,' she said. 'Do make yourselves at home.'

By the time she came downstairs Gary and Dean had indeed made themselves at home. Dean was watching the snooker on Linda's dodgy telly while Gary was flicking through Linda's large pile of photo albums. He sprang to his feet apologetically when Linda entered the room.

'Hope you don't mind me peeking at your pics, love,' he said.

Startled, Linda peered over his shoulder to see what he was looking at. The album was open at a picture of Kate sitting on her dad's knee when she was about four. She'd had her face painted to look like a purple butterfly and was grinning fit to burst.

'Well no,' said Linda. 'I suppose not. Not really.'

Still not sure whether she was doing the right thing, she

perched on the side of the settee as Dean went through his list of questions.

'Where does Kate go to school?'

'Has she got any hobbies?'

'Who's her favourite pop star?'

'What present will she buy you if she wins Starspotter?'

'What does her dad think about her being in the final?'

Linda answered everything as truthfully as she could. The only query she baulked at was the one about Ray, her ex-husband and Kate's dad. It wasn't any of Gary and Dean's business that Ray hadn't been in touch for years. She didn't have a clue where he was.

'I … I'd rather Kate's dad wasn't brought into it,' said Linda. 'D'you mind?'

'Sure,' Dean agreed readily. 'No problem.'

After twenty minutes or so, Dean seemed content with what he'd got and Gary began taking pictures. This was the bit that Linda had been dreading but it was over in a trice. Gary took a couple of snaps of her holding a picture of Kate, then a few more of her standing on the front step and that was it, he was done.

'What paper will this be in?' Linda called out as the two men crossed the street to the car.

Dean shrugged his shoulders nonchalantly.

'Dunno, love,' he said. 'We'll let you know.'

And with that, they both jumped into the car and roared away.

15
Out on the Lake

K ATE ROLLED over to check the illuminated display on the clock beside her bed. She groaned when she saw how late it was. Blast. Blast. Blast. Ten past nine already.

Why hadn't she been sensible last night and gone to sleep earlier? Dottie had shooed them all up to bed at a respectable ten p.m. The trouble was that when the coast was clear Kate and the four other finalists had sneaked up to Astoria's room for a midnight feast.

It had been Scooter's idea, of course. The instant Astoria let slip that her dad had packed her a secret stash of chocolate to see her through the next two weeks Scooter had leapt on it like a terrier.

'Come on, let's have a party in the attic,' he giggled. 'No one will hear us up there. It'll be wicked.'

Sophy and Scooter had brought along yet more sweets and fizzy drinks while Tommy sheepishly produced a Victoria sponge cake his mum had baked for him.

'She was worried they might not give us enough to eat,' he explained. 'Sorry it's a bit squashed.'

To her intense mortification, Kate didn't have anything to add to the feast.

'Maybe it's best if I don't come,' she told the others. 'It wouldn't be fair – seeing as I can't put in my share.'

Astonishingly it was Astoria who put her arm round Kate's shoulder and insisted that it didn't matter in the least.

'We've got loads already,' she whispered in Kate's ear. 'We'll be sick if we eat all this lot. And just imagine if that happened and we couldn't rehearse next week. Daniel Drewsome would go off his trolley.'

Lying in bed, Kate grinned as she recalled Astoria's kindness of the night before. Astoria was weird. One minute she was behaving atrociously, bragging about how brilliant she was and complaining that the girls' dormitory wasn't nearly luxurious enough. The next she was going out of her way to be super-kind and considerate.

'I don't understand her at all,' Kate mumbled to herself, still half asleep. 'Will the real Astoria Lennox please stand up?'

The sound of Dottie crashing into the room and bellowing at the two girls to get out of bed cut through Kate's day-dreaming.

'Come on you horrible lot,' Dottie yelled. 'Jump to it. You've got breakfast in twenty minutes. And then at ten-thirty we're off on a jaunt. Get cracking for goodness' sake. You've had a lot more beauty sleep than I have.'

Judging by the looks on everyone else's faces at breakfast, they felt just as bad as Kate, if not worse. Scooter and Tommy both had dark circles round their eyes while Sophy could scarcely keep her eyes open long enough to eat her porridge. Astoria was like a bear with a sore head. Being deprived of her usual eight hours' sleep had made her so tetchy that she snapped at everyone the moment they dared open their mouths.

'Blooming Nora, you're going to have to cope an awful lot better than this,' Dottie reprimanded them crossly. 'You've only been here for five minutes and you can't take the pace. Just wait till GG and Garcia get into their stride with you next week. You ain't seen nothing yet, kiddos.'

Garcia was fine – he was a real sweetie – but each of

them shuddered at the prospect of GG 'getting into her stride.' Surely the dance teacher couldn't be any scarier than she'd been last week?

Dottie instructed the group to assemble in the hall at ten-thirty, dressed in scruffy clothes and trainers.

'And don't forget to collect a picnic from the kitchen,' she ordered.

'We're not little kids,' mumbled Scooter. 'You don't have to treat us as if we're five years old.'

'Don't I? Well, you could have fooled me.'

By ten-forty, however, only Sophy and Kate had arrived. Dottie, who was dressed in a weird all-in-one jumpsuit the colour of lemon sherbet, lost her temper.

'What *is* the matter with you lot today?' she screeched at the two girls. 'I don't know why I bother.'

Then, seeing Kate and Sophy's dejected faces she was overcome with remorse.

'Oh I know it's unreasonable of me to take it out on you. You two are the only ones who've actually made the effort to get here on time. It's the others who are a lazy bunch of layabouts. Where the blooming heck are they?'

It was eleven by the time Tommy, Scooter and Astoria eventually drifted downstairs. Dottie was now incandescent with fury. Kate had never seen her look so cross. She was so red in the face Kate thought she might explode.

'You're going to have to learn to get your act together,' raged Dottie. 'It is so unprofessional to be late. And rude. And ungrateful. And ... And ... Oh, what's the point? Maybe Daniel was right. If he'd had his way you'd have been in a dance rehearsal with GG at the crack of dawn. It was me who persuaded him to relent and give you Sunday off. I shouldn't have been so soft.'

Even Scooter, who never seemed bothered by anything, was contrite.

122

'We're really, really sorry, Dottie,' he said. His voice sounded full of remorse, but he was such a joker that no one was sure it was genuine or not. 'Will you forgive us if we promise to behave like angels from now on?'

'And pigs might fly,' said Dottie gruffly. 'Don't push your luck, pal. But OK, I'll forgive you this time. Just make sure you're not late again. Or I really will go potty.'

Ken, the minibus driver, laughed when he saw the five youngsters meekly trotting behind Dottie.

'You've got this lot licked into shape pretty quick, girl,' he told her. 'They were a right rowdy crew the other day and now they look as if butter wouldn't melt in their mouths. Will you have a go at sorting out my kids for me? My Ryan's a right cheeky so-and-so and Connor doesn't take a blind bit of notice of anything I say. What d'you reckon? Is it a deal?'

'In a word, Ken,' said Dottie, her voice icy. 'No. It is not a deal. I've got enough on my plate with *this* horrible bunch, thank you very much. My hair will be grey by the time the competition's over.'

The group clambered on to the minibus, careful to leave the front seat for Dottie. They'd been in enough trouble for one day. They didn't want to antagonise her further.

Just as Ken put the minibus into gear, ready to accelerate up the Starspotter Academy's long bumpy drive, there was a tap on the passenger window. It was Sean, *Rise and Shine*'s chief cameraman. He was out of breath, puffing and panting as if he'd just run a four-minute mile.

Dottie wound down her window to talk to him.

'What d'you want? We're running late enough as it is.'

''Fraid we're coming too, Dot,' wheezed Sean. 'I know it's not what you want to hear right now, but Daniel's just texted me to say he wants shots of the kids on the water.

123

That man will be the death of me. It's my first day off all week. I was just tucking into a mega fry-up.'

Kate, who was sitting directly behind Dottie, sat bolt upright at this. On the water? What on earth did Sean mean?

'Why is Daniel such a blooming pain?' grumbled Dottie. 'He told me quite clearly after the show that the kids could have a break today. Recharge their batteries ready for next week.'

'Sorry Dot,' said Sean, beckoning to the rest of the crew to follow him. 'You know how it is. When the boss says "jump" you jump. Know what I mean?'

Dottie sat fuming in the passenger seat as Sean and his three colleagues hauled their gear – cameras, audio equipment and all – into the back of the minibus. By the time the four men had climbed on board too, there was barely room to breathe.

'You don't exactly travel light, do you?' Dottie grumbled. 'We'll be hard pressed to get up the drive with this lot.'

'Sorry, Dot,' said Sean once more.

'And don't flaming well call me Dot,' snapped Dottie.

It was OK for Daniel, she thought, as Sean squeezed in between her and Ken. He'd disappeared back to the plush Brackenside Hotel directly after Saturday's show, leaving her to pick up the pieces. Just like he always did.

As the minibus trundled up the track towards the village of Lakevale, Dottie's mood began to lift.

She gazed up at the tops of the bracken-covered fells. They were blanketed in mist yet she didn't care a hoot. She simply felt relieved to have escaped from the confines of the Starspotter Academy. How ridiculous to get things so out of proportion. Over the last few days she had forgotten there was a world outside *The Rise and Shine*

Saturday Show. It was only a telly programme after all. Dottie made a secret vow to herself not to get in such a stew in future. Oh, and before the end of the competition she was going to climb one of those mountains if it was the last thing she did.

Even though it was July and the rest of the country was now basking in a heatwave, raindrops began to splatter on the windscreen of the minibus.

'I wondered when that would happen,' grumbled Sean. 'You know that the Lake District is renowned for being the wettest place in Britain. It's going to ruin my filming.'

'D'you want to stop for the Sunday papers?' Ken asked Dottie, trying to change the subject. He didn't take kindly to soft southerners moaning about his birthplace.

'You what?' said Dottie. 'Oh yes. Good idea. I really ought to check if any of them have done stuff on yesterday's *Rise and Shine*.'

'Right you are,' said Ken, braking sharply outside Lakevale's one and only shop.

The scruffy wooden sign outside Vale Stores boasted that it sold everything from Kendal mint cake to firelighters. And sure enough, a large array of Sunday newspapers were arranged in a rack by the front door, along with assorted colour postcards of the Lake District, logs, kindling and bags of charcoal.

Dottie grabbed a copy of every paper on the stand and disappeared inside to pay for them. When she emerged a couple of minutes later she was grinning from ear to ear.

'Kate,' she yelled as she climbed back into the minibus. 'You'll never guess who's on the front page of the *Sunday Mirror* and the *Mail on Sunday*…'

Kate didn't reply. She was miles away, singing along to a Joss Stone track on Sophy's iPod.

Sophy elbowed Kate in the ribs and pulled the headphones off her friend.

'Hey, I was listening to that,' protested Kate, trying to snatch them back again.

'Dottie's trying to talk to you.'

Kate looked up and caught Dottie's eye.

'Look at this, Kate,' said Dottie, waving the newspapers at her. 'And this. You and your mum have only blooming gone and hit the front pages. Bet you've never done that before.'

For a second Kate couldn't think what on earth Dottie was on about. She grabbed hold of the *Sunday Mirror* and gazed at the front page, completely flabbergasted.

'W... what ... how?' she spluttered.

The front page of the *Sunday Mirror* was dominated by some boring political story or other. But slap bang in the centre of the page was a huge colour picture of Kate and Garcia Andrew singing their TV duet. And emblazoned across the top of the picture in big letters were the words: *STARSPOTTER KATE'S HAPPY BIRTHDAY TO MUM!*

Kate simply couldn't get her head round it at all.

'I don't understand, I don't understand,' she kept saying over and over again. 'What are me and Garcia doing in the *Sunday Mirror*?'

'And that's not all,' chuckled Dottie, passing the *Mail on Sunday* across. 'You're on the front page of this as well!'

The *Mail on Sunday* had used exactly the same picture – but with the caption *MY MUM'S THE BEST!*

Sophy, Scooter, Tommy and Astoria all peered over Kate's shoulder to look at the papers.

'*Lancashire lass Kate Barnsley teamed up with chart-topper Garcia Andrew to sing a birthday tribute to her mum on national TV yesterday,*' read Scooter, putting on his best BBC newscaster's voice. '*Kate, thirteen, is one of the five young finalists on* The Rise and Shine Saturday Show'*s Starspotter competition. Her mum Linda was in tears at home in*

Gribblesdale, Lancashire, as she watched Kate wish her a happy 35th birthday.

' "It's the best birthday present I've ever had," said single mum Linda, a hard-up factory worker. "I knew my Kate wouldn't forget."

'The five Starspotter youngsters are ensconced in a hideaway in the Lake District, competing to win a record contract ... bla bla bla ...'

'Wow,' said Sophy. She turned to Kate, her eyes shining with excitement. 'You're famous now.'

'Don't be soft,' protested Kate. 'They must be short of proper news to put me and Garcia on the front page.'

'I don't believe it,' said Tommy. 'I never thought one of us would be in the papers. It's fantastic!'

'Just enjoy it, Kate,' smiled Dottie. 'Your mum'll be over the moon, won't she?'

The shock of seeing herself in two national newspapers was only just starting to sink in. Kate wasn't sure *what* her mum would think.

'Oooh, I don't know. Nothing like this has ever happened to us before.'

Dottie reached over and patted Kate's hand reassuringly.

'Well, it has now,' she said. 'But don't take it too much to heart – those papers'll be fish and chip wrappings this time tomorrow.'

The only person on the minibus who hadn't said a word in all the commotion was Astoria. Dottie knew perfectly well why. The pure and simple fact was that Astoria was green with envy, livid that it was Kate in the papers and not her.

All thoughts of the *Sunday Mirror* coverage were forgotten when the minibus turned a sharp right out of Lakevale and headed down a lane signposted Valewater Cruises.

Kate's mood changed abruptly when she spotted the sign. A trickle of fear ran down her spine and her heart began beating wildly. What had Dottie got planned?

'You should have called this trip "Dottie's Magical Mystery Tour,"' laughed Scooter. 'Can't you tell us where you're taking us?'

'You'll have to be patient for a little while longer,' said Dottie. 'But don't worry. I promise it'll be fun. Mark my words. You'll all have a whale of a time.'

Ken drew up outside a large wooden building with *Valewater Cruises* emblazoned across the front. Beyond it was a tiny marina, with scores of dinghies and motor cruisers moored side by side.

The rigging on the dinghies clinked noisily against the masts. There hadn't been a breath of wind in Lakevale but down by the water there was a sharp breeze.

Kate shivered with fear. Surely they weren't going sailing?

Sophy let out a screech of excitement at the sight of the boats.

'Being by the water reminds me of home,' she shrieked. 'Which one's ours?'

'Calm down, Sophy,' soothed Dottie. 'You are *not* crewing a boat. No, we're all going on a nice, relaxing cruise round Lake Valewater. Then we'll have a picnic on the tiny island in the middle of the lake. Look, over there. Can you see it? They used to keep prisoners on it during the war.'

Kate sighed with relief. For one awful moment she'd thought they were doing something *really* scary, canoeing maybe, or sailing. But a trip round the lake on a motor cruiser didn't sound too daunting. She could cope with that.

The truth was that Kate could barely swim a stroke and was terrified of water. Her dad had tried – not very patiently – to teach her when she was little, but she simply couldn't get the hang of it. Week after week he'd taken her to Gribblesdale Public Baths, bellowing at her like a foghorn from the side as she struggled to stay afloat. But the lessons had been no use. After he'd left home, Kate had set her mind against swimming completely, avoiding it at all costs. In year four at primary school, swimming lessons had been compulsory, but somehow or other Kate nearly always managed to get out of them. One week she'd forget her swimming things, another she'd persuade her mum she had a cold and couldn't go.

Two young men hurried out of the wooden shack to meet them. They looked like twins with their short blond hair and weather-beaten complexions. They were both kitted out in wet suits, navy Valewater Cruises sweat shirts and identical Rayban sunglasses perched on their heads.

'Hi,' said the slightly taller of the two. 'I'm Ned Lister. You must be Dottie and the Starspotter gang.'

'Sounds like a rock group,' laughed the other man, shaking Dottie firmly by the hand. 'And I'm Kit Lister, by the way. We're brothers.'

'I'd never have guessed,' laughed Dottie. 'We're really looking forward to our cruise. Have you got life jackets sorted out for us?'

'Sure have,' said Ned. 'We wouldn't let you on the boat without them. Come on kids, let's get you sorted.'

Five minutes later, the Starspotter youngsters hurried along the jetty, all wearing matching bright orange life jackets over their clothes.

'You look really hilarious, Astoria,' teased Scooter. 'Bright orange really isn't your colour, is it? I bet you regret choosing that purple outfit of yours now.'

Astoria glared at Scooter. It was on the tip of her tongue to make a scathing remark about his *Robbie Williams* T-shirt – how seriously uncool was that? But she suddenly realised that Sean, the *Rise and Shine* cameraman, was filming their conversation and her scowl instantly transformed itself into a wide smile.

'This is so exciting, isn't it, Scooter?' she gushed, flicking her blonde curls over her shoulder.

'You what?' said Scooter. He gaped at Astoria. He'd been expecting a biting remark in return.

Astoria glanced over at Sean once more and saw that he had now turned his attention to Sophy, who was happily skimming stones across the water.

'Get lost, you berk,' she seethed at the hapless Scooter.

Kate took a deep breath and followed Dottie gingerly along the jetty, trying hard not to look down. At the end of the pier Ned and Kit stood waiting for them alongside their pride and joy, a sleek open top cruiser called *Lady Christina*. As the group approached, Ned held out a tanned muscular arm to help them on board.

Once again, Kate concentrated hard as she stepped from the wooden jetty on to the boat, grabbing hold of Ned's hand to steady herself. She was desperate to hide her fear but Ned could see how nervous she was.

'You all right, sweetheart?' he asked quietly.

'Yep. I'm OK. Really I am. Absolutely great. Can't wait.'

Kate knew she was gabbling but she couldn't help it. She made her way along the rows of seats and sat down hurriedly alongside Dottie.

'Are you all right, Kate?' asked Dottie, concerned. 'You look a tiny bit green.'

'I'm fine,' lied Kate. 'Really. Just feeling a tiny bit sick, that's all.'

'I know what you mean. I must tell Ken to take those corners a bit more gently on the way home. We don't want you throwing up all over the place. The pace is really going to intensify over the next ten days. You've got to be on tip-top form.'

At last everyone was on board and Kit started up the engine. Kate let out a tiny yelp of fear but tried to muffle it by coughing loudly.

Dottie regarded her suspiciously once again but Kate pretended not to notice. She gripped the bar in front more tightly than ever.

Sophy, Astoria, Scooter and Tommy were having the time of their lives at the front of the boat. It was surprisingly choppy on the water and the further out they got the higher the waves lashed against *Lady Christina*'s bow. The impact of the waves hitting the boat sent water spraying over the front passengers. Sophy and Tommy were soon wet through.

'I think I'd better move nearer the front to keep an eye on them,' murmured Dottie, getting to her feet.

Anxious not to be left by herself, Kate got up to follow her.

'I'm coming with you,' she said hurriedly.

The pair made their way down the aisle to join the others, who were all laughing uproariously. Astoria and Scooter were both soaked to the bone as well now, but no one was in the least bothered.

'Kate, come and stand over here with us,' shouted Sophy as another wave engulfed her. 'It's really fun.'

Before Kate knew what was happening, Sophy had grabbed hold of her and she was standing at the bow.

'You look like Rose on the *Titanic*,' joked Scooter.

On a normal day Kate would have been flattered by his remark but right now she was too terrified to reply. All she could think about was the expanse of water stretching before her as far as the eye could see.

'Please let it be time to land on the island,' she prayed silently to herself. 'Please, please, please.'

At that moment a massive wave swept over the boat and drenched the youngsters. While the others clapped their hands and screamed out in excitement, Kate stood frozen to the spot in sheer terror. Disorientated, her hands let go of the rail and when a second wave hit the boat seconds later, she slipped sideways into the icy water.

16
Ned to the Rescue

EVERYTHING HAPPENED so fast that it was hard to make sense of it. Just about the only certainty was that within seconds of Kate plunging overboard Ned had hurtled down the boat like a rocket. He dived headfirst into the lake and began powering through the water towards Kate.

Lake Valewater had always looked so crystal-clear and inviting when viewed from the safety of the Starspotter Academy. But now the sky had darkened to a charcoal grey and the waves crashed against the side of the boat like wild animals.

'I've done a life saving course at school,' yelled Tommy, wrenching off his life jacket, jeans and trainers and chucking them on the deck. 'He might need help. I'm going in too.'

'*No, you are not,*' bellowed Dottie, her voice tight with fear. 'Do you hear me, Tommy? *Stay right where you are.*'

But Tommy didn't take any notice. He clambered on to the bow of the boat and jumped straight in after Ned.

A piercing scream from Sophy ripped through the air. The Scots girl could hardly bear to watch the scene unfolding in front of her. First Kate, now Tommy. It was Kate she was most scared about, though. Her friend's life jacket would keep her buoyant for a while – Sophy knew that – but she looked so panic-stricken, thrashing about and gulping for air.

'She's going to be fine,' shouted Dottie, barely aware of

what she was yelling but knowing she had to say *something* to calm everyone down. This trip was enough of a catastrophe already without Sophy going into hysterics. 'Look, Ned and Tommy have almost got hold of her now.'

At that very moment Ned grabbed Kate, flipping seamlessly on to his back and cradling her lifeless form against him. Then, with Tommy alongside to help support her head, the pair of them swam slowly back to the boat.

Kit, who had stopped the engine when the commotion began, was leaning over the side to help his brother hoist Kate back on board. No one uttered a word. They were too horrified to speak.

Kate looked in a dreadful state. White-faced and spluttering with shock, she collapsed into Dottie's arms, then promptly spewed out a torrent of lake water all over the deck. Dottie didn't bat an eyelid. She seized a large picnic blanket and wrapped the shivering, petrified teenager in it.

'There, there,' she whispered soothingly. 'I've got you. You're safe and sound now, sweetheart. Don't worry about a thing. We'll get you warm in a jiffy. You've had the most terrible fright but everything's going to be fine.'

'Kit has radioed for an ambulance,' Ned whispered to Dottie. 'There's a rescue team based near Lakevale and they've been scrambled too.'

'Thank goodness,' said Dottie, relieved that the two brothers had reacted so fast and help was on its way. 'I don't know what we'd have done if you hadn't rescued her so quickly. She could have drowned out there.'

Deep down, Dottie felt desperately anxious. Not for herself – though as the leading member of the *Rise and Shine* team present she was technically responsible for the youngsters' safety – but for Kate. The girl was clearly in a bad way.

Everyone remained deathly quiet during the fifteen minutes it took the *Lady Christina* to speed back to the marina. All the colour had drained from Astoria's face and for once even the ebullient Scooter was silent.

As the boat drew close to the jetty Dottie caught sight of the ambulance waiting for them on the shore, its blue light flashing. She nearly wept with relief.

The instant the motor cruiser docked, two paramedics in bright green uniforms rushed on board. Within seconds they'd established exactly what had happened, lifted Kate on to a stretcher and carried her into the ambulance. Dottie bellowed at Tommy to follow her – he'd been in the freezing water for several minutes and she wanted him checked out by the hospital too.

'Don't worry, we'll ring the academy and tell them what's happened,' Kit reassured Dottie as she clambered into the ambulance. 'The other kids can wait with us till someone comes to collect them.'

Tears trickled down Sophy's cheeks as the ambulance roared off in the direction of Lakevale. She watched the blue light flashing till it disappeared out of sight, keeping her fingers crossed tightly behind her back. Please, please let Kate be all right.

Ned was puzzled by the way Sophy kept muttering to herself.

'Are you sure you're OK?'

'This is all my fault, completely my fault,' Sophy wailed over and over again. 'It was me who pulled her up to the front. She didn't want to. She really didn't. She just froze when the waves hit the boat. But I didn't have any idea she was so scared of water.'

'None of us did,' said Ned quietly. 'Don't beat yourself up over this, love. It wasn't anyone's fault. It was a freak accident – no one could have predicted it.

135

Your friend is going to be just fine. Believe me. She really is.'

Ned was right. Two hours later, Kate was sitting up in bed at Lakeside General Hospital, bright-eyed and bushy-tailed. She seemed none the worse for her ordeal, although the young doctor who'd examined her said she was suffering from shock and mild hypothermia and would have to stay in overnight for observation.

'Don't worry about it,' he said. 'You'll be as right as rain. And I promise you'll be able to go home in the morning.'

The mention of the word 'home' sent Kate into a panic.

'What does he mean?' she asked Dottie in an anxious voice. 'I *can't* go home. I just can't. Not to Gribblesdale, I mean. He's made a mistake. I *can* go back to the Starspotter Academy, can't I? Tell me I can.'

Dottie sighed inwardly. She hadn't left Kate's side all afternoon but she could see there was trouble ahead. And from the way Kate's bottom lip was wobbling it was obvious that what she was about to tell her wouldn't go down well.

'Kate,' began Dottie gently.

'What?'

Dottie swallowed hard. There was no easy way to put this.

'You know how gruelling it is at the academy,' she went on. 'You said yourself that the voice and dance lessons have been far more demanding than you expected. I hate having to say this but you've just had the most terrifying experience. If the doctor says you must go home and convalesce for a few days, then that's what you have to do. For your own good. Your health is far more important than a silly pop competition. Surely you can see that, sweetheart?'

Kate stared uncomprehendingly at Dottie. Her face was still deathly white and she wore a white cotton hospital robe at least two sizes too big for her. She looked more like six than thirteen.

'...And then I can come back to the academy,' insisted Kate firmly. 'I'll have a couple of days at home, put my feet up and stuff... Let Mum look after me. And then I can carry on with the competition... I can, can't I, Dottie? Say I can.'

Dottie stared up at the ceiling. The white paint was peeling off in the far corner. How could she explain this to Kate? How could she explain that by the time she was well enough to return the others would be a million miles ahead with their singing and dancing? They'd really show her up. The grand final was next Saturday and she wouldn't stand a cat's chance in hell. It would be like making a five-year-old compete against Madonna.

But Dottie didn't have the heart to say all this to Kate. 'Blooming heck,' she thought, 'the poor kid nearly drowned out there – I can't dash her hopes by banning her from the competition now.'

'So when I'm better I can come back?' persisted Kate.

'Maybe,' said Dottie weakly. 'We'll just have to wait and see.'

As Dottie expected, Daniel Drewsome had gone stark raving bonkers when he found out what had happened on the lake.

Even though she had rung him from the hospital to tell him about the accident, she wasn't sure whether he'd turn up to see Kate or not. But as she left the ward to ring Linda Barnsley and give her an update on Kate's progress, Daniel came hurtling down the corridor at high speed. He looked livid, his jet-black hair sticking up on end and his face an alarming shade of purple.

'How could you let such a thing happen?' he raged at Dottie. 'How could you be so stupid?'

Dottie stared at her boss. The way he was ranting and raving you'd have thought she'd engineered the whole thing on purpose.

'I'm as upset as you are,' she said. 'It was terrible out there. The poor girl was in such a state, I was really scared she might drown.'

'Is…is she OK?' he spluttered.

'I thought you'd never ask,' said Dottie coldly. 'But yes, thank goodness, she is. She's suffering from shock – and mild hypothermia. The doctors are planning to keep her in tonight but she should be well enough to go back to Lancashire tomorrow.'

Daniel gaped at her.

'Lancashire? What do you mean, Lancashire?'

'It's where Kate lives, of course. I'm just about to ring her mum to tell her the good news. Unless you want to do it? It might be better coming from you.'

Daniel looked utterly appalled at this prospect. Dealing with contestants' mums was *not* his thing. Not by a long chalk.

'No, no, that's your department, Dottie,' he said hurriedly. 'But you *will* be careful, won't you? You know how litigious people are these days. We don't want the Barnsley woman suing us for not taking sufficient care of her daughter. We're *in loco parentis* here, you know.'

This was the last thing on Dottie's mind.

'The only thing Linda Barnsley is going to be bothered about is that Kate's all right,' she said. 'Call me soft but as a matter of fact it's the only thing *I* care about too.'

'And tell her not to go to the papers,' said Daniel. 'We don't want a word of this getting out. They'll stitch us up like a kipper if it does.'

Kate slept badly that night, tossing and turning till the early hours. Dottie had stayed with her till the nurses chucked her out at eight p.m. but after that she'd been on her own.

'I'll be back in the morning,' Dottie had promised, blowing her a kiss from the end of the ward. 'And your mum should be here by then too, you know. Daniel's organised for a car to pick her up at the crack of dawn and bring her straight here. She's desperate to see you. You know that, don't you?'

When Kate woke at seven the next morning she could scarcely believe her eyes. Her mother was watching her from a chair at the side of her bed. Linda was wearing faded jeans and an old fleece that had once been scarlet but was now a dusky shade of pink. She looked thin and pale and desperately anxious.

'*Mum*,' shrieked Kate, clambering out of bed to give her a hug. 'I can't believe you're here.'

'Oh love,' cried Linda, tears coursing down her cheeks. 'I'm so relieved to see you. I've been that worried about you. Honestly, if that *Rise and Shine* car hadn't arrived to pick me up this morning I swear I would have run all the way here. Are you sure you're all right? That Dottie should have known better. She should have taken better care of you. I trusted her.'

But Kate wouldn't hear a word of criticism against Dottie.

'She wasn't to blame, Mum. Truly she wasn't. Everyone said it was a freak accident, even the boat people. It could have happened to anyone. It was my own stupid fault really. If only I wasn't such a hopeless swimmer. I just happened to be in the wrong place at the wrong time.'

'Hmmm…I'm not so sure,' said Linda. 'But if that's what you say I'll have to take your word for it. And thank heaven you're OK. I knew I shouldn't have let you enter that silly Starspotter competition. I should never have let you persuade me. I can't think what possessed me. Well, at least it's over now. We can go home and get back to normal. Sally's on holiday with her mum and dad but she's kept calling for news of how you've been getting on. And Gwenda Graham at the newsagent's says she can't manage without you. She was dead chuffed at the picture of us in the papers yesterday. Even brought me round a couple of complementary copies, she did!'

For now, Kate didn't argue. Everyone – the doctors, Dottie, her mum – seemed to be in complete agreement about her convalescing at home. She didn't have the energy to kick up a fuss now. She'd have to start working on her mum once they were back in Bright Street.

Linda didn't leave Kate's side for a second during the next three hours. She was content simply to sit and watch her daughter drift in and out of sleep, relieved that she'd come out of the drama unscathed.

Soon after ten a.m., the doctors did their ward round and pronounced that Kate was fit and well enough to go home.

'But how will we get back to Gribblesdale?' Kate asked her mum. 'Have you checked the train times? And what am I going to wear? I don't know what's happened to my clothes. They were all soaking wet when I arrived. That's why I'm wearing this horrible thing.'

Linda laughed out loud.

'So many questions, love. You *must* be on the mend. The driver who brought me up here is waiting in reception. He's from Gribblesdale Cabs. He could hardly believe his luck to get a job like this. Most of the time he's back and forth to the chippy or the station.'

'And my clothes?' said Kate again, glancing down at her shapeless hospital gown. 'I can't go home in this. The whole street would laugh their heads off.'

Linda fished a battered holdall from underneath the bed.

'Don't worry, sweetheart. I thought of that. I've brought you a fresh set.'

At that moment Dottie popped her head anxiously round the curtain of Kate's cubicle. When she saw Kate chatting animatedly to Linda, her face lit up.

'Oh Kate, I can't tell you how wonderful it is to see the colour back in your cheeks. Honestly, I haven't been so relieved since Sophie Ellis Bextor beat Posh Spice to number one. You look a different girl to yesterday. You had me so worried.'

'You and me both,' murmured Linda. 'I trusted you, Dottie. I can't think how you could have let such a thing happen...'

'Stop it, Mum,' said Kate firmly. She was not going to let *anyone*, not even Linda, utter a word of criticism against Dottie. 'I told you before. None of this was Dottie's fault. Like I said, if it was anyone's fault it was mine. I should have had more sense than to go up to the front like that. *And* I should have taken more notice of Dad when he tried to teach me to swim.'

The reference to Ray completely took the wind out of Linda's sails. She hadn't heard Kate mention her father for years.

'All right,' said Linda grudgingly. 'I'm sorry, Dottie. It's just that I've been that worried...'

'We all have,' said Dottie in a quiet voice.

The two women and Kate gazed at the floor, uncertain what to say next. The moment of awkwardness was swept aside in a flash, however, by the sound of clattering heels racing down the ward.

The curtain was yanked back, and there, clutching the most enormous teddy bear Kate had ever seen, stood Zaza.

Actually, Kate had to bite the insides of her cheeks to stop herself bursting out laughing. The *Rise and Shine* presenter looked completely out of place in the austere ward. For a start Zaza was wearing the tiniest pink mini skirt Kate had ever seen, along with pink and black spotty tights and a pink crop top that showed off her tiny waist. Her blonde hair was caught back in a pink velvet ribbon and she tottered precariously on four-inch platforms.

'Hiya,' shrieked Zaza and lurched forward to give Kate a huge hug.

Linda gaped in astonishment, especially when Zaza was followed into the cubicle by a concerned-looking Sean and the rest of the TV crew, all carrying bunches of white tulips, roses and lily of the valley.

'These are for you, love,' said Sean gruffly, thrusting the flowers at Kate. 'I've got kids of my own and … well, me and the lads have been worried about you.'

'And this is a special get well present from me,' giggled Zaza, handing the gigantic teddy to Kate. 'He's called Zazou – after me, of course. Oh, and this … oh, where is it?'

Zaza frowned as she fumbled in her bag for what she was looking for.

'Here it is,' she said, her face brightening. 'This is a little something from Didi. And, sweetie-pie, *little* really is the word for it.'

Zaza handed the bewildered Kate a minuscule box of chocolates. Linda noticed that the gift was slightly crumpled and decidedly on the mingy side compared to that magnificent teddy – but she suspected that this was precisely what Zaza had intended.

Even the normally chatty Dottie was lost for words as Zaza prattled away about nothing in particular. Dottie hadn't managed to get much sleep the night before and Zaza seemed to be making even less sense than usual.

When Zaza and the crew finally swept out of the ward ten minutes later, hotly pursued by a gaggle of autograph hunters, Linda turned to Kate and sighed with fatigue.

'D'you know what?' she asked Kate.

'What?'

'I don't know about you but I've just about had enough of *Rise and Shine* for one day. It's like having a walk-on part in one of the telly soaps. It's time I took you back to Gribblesdale, young lady.'

17
Astoria Makes a Friend

IT WAS ten past six on Wednesday night, three days after Kate's accident. Scooter and Tommy were lounging around on the sofa in Dottie's room watching *The Simpsons*. Sophy was writing a postcard in her room and Astoria had sneaked down to the ballroom to practise her dance routines once more. Scooter had accused her of being 'teacher's pet' but she couldn't care less. She was determined to impress GG with her body-popping if it was the last thing she did.

She was halfway through the trickiest bit when Didi put her head round the door.

'Have you seen Daniel anywhere? We're supposed to be going out for a meal. Not that there's anywhere decent to eat in this dump.'

Astoria sped across to the CD player and turned the volume down.

'Sorry, no. He hardly ever comes over here unless he has to.'

'No worries,' said Didi. 'Hey, that dancing of yours looks as though it's coming on a treat by the way. How are you lot doing?'

'Not too bad,' said Astoria. She was out of breath but determined not to show it. 'I wish we weren't so far away from everywhere though. It's so quiet here. I miss London, even the traffic and the pollution.'

'Join the club,' murmured Didi. 'I'm definitely not sticking around here after this week's show. I need to

144

touch base with my London self.'

Astoria wasn't sure what Didi meant by this but she was impressed all the same. If only she could be half as sophisticated as Didi. The presenter looked so cool in her skin-tight jeans and slinky purple vest – far better than that dippy Zaza girl.

'That's exactly what I think,' said Astoria. 'The rest of the finalists are so … so … jokey. They're always having a laugh and they don't take anything seriously. I mean, we're here to work, aren't we? Maybe it'd be better if Kate was still around. I think she's a bit more determined than the others.'

Actually Astoria didn't want Kate back at all. Astoria had been green with envy when Kate's picture was splashed all over the papers and scared stiff that she might win the competition. She posed far too much of a threat.

'Oh I wouldn't worry your pretty head about that,' chuckled Didi. 'Kate's quite a Mummy's girl and her mum has told Daniel that she'll be back over her dead body. She was livid about Kate falling in the water like that. Poor diddums. No way is she coming back to the academy.'

Astoria smirked with satisfaction. This was the best news she'd had all day. The best all week come to think of it.

Didi eyed Astoria with interest. Up until tonight she had lumped the entire Starspotter gang together, privately sneering at them as 'boring mini wannabes' who'd be after her job in a few years time. But Astoria, she could see, was a girl after her own heart – cool, talented and, when it came to getting her own way, utterly ruthless.

Didi was well aware too, that Zaza secretly had a soft spot for the idiotic Scooter. It was perfectly plain her co-presenter thought the youngster was hilarious because she burst into great peals of laughter every time Scooter cracked one of his pathetic jokes. And she'd even admitted to Didi in private that Scooter was bound to charm the birds off the trees when it came to the phone vote.

'All the mums and grannies will love him,' Zaza had giggled.

Right, thought Didi as she stood chatting to Astoria. If Zaza was going to have a favourite, then so was she. And *she* was going to champion Astoria. At least this girl looked a real winner. In fact she quite liked the idea of having a little protégé to offer advice and fashion tips to.

'What have you got on your schedule for tomorrow?' Didi demanded.

A puzzled look appeared on Astoria's face.

'Schedule? I'm not sure what you mean. Everyday seems the same here.'

Didi frowned with impatience. Maybe Astoria wasn't so bright after all.

'I mean … Honestly sweetie, it's not rocket science. What classes have you got tomorrow?'

Didi spoke slowly and precisely, enunciating her words as if she was addressing someone who couldn't understand English very well.

'O-hhhh,' said Astoria, cottoning on at last. She took a crumpled piece of paper out of her pocket.

'Wednesday,' she said, reading aloud. 'We start off with …'

'No,' bellowed Didi. 'It's Thursday tomorrow, you nincompoop. What's on the schedule for Thursday?'

Seeing Didi's irritation, Astoria cursed herself.

'Oh, er, er right. We start off with a two-hour dance class with GG at nine. Then we get a break for half an hour and after that we're doing interview techniques with Daniel. So we're ready for our chat with you and Zaza on Saturday. We get an hour for lunch and then we're going to be practising the songs for this week's *Rise and Shine* with Garcia.'

'Hmmm,' said Didi, thinking hard. 'And exactly how much do you want to win this show, Astoria?'

Astoria stared at Didi. What an idiotic question. It was like asking a dog if it wanted a bone. Not that dogs could talk, of course.

'About a million zillion times a million. That's why I'm here, isn't it?'

'That's more like it,' said Didi, nodding her head approvingly. 'Now this is the plan. If you do exactly what I say you'll win Starspotter and you'll be a million zillion times more famous than the others. So listen very carefully and follow my instructions to the letter … Got it?'

Up in the girls' dorm, Sophy was missing Kate like mad. Every time she glanced across at Kate's bed, covered in its pink and lime duvet and neatly piled up with the belongings she'd left behind, she felt like bursting into tears.

Starspotter simply wasn't the same without Kate. Sophy had been getting along fine with Tommy and Scooter over the past few days – and even Astoria was just about bearable – but Kate was her *friend*. The two girls had so much in common. They both *loved* Robbie Williams and the Black Eyed Peas and thought Westlife were rubbish. They both reckoned chicken tikka masala was wicked and boiled eggs and salami were gross. They both preferred skinny jeans to skirts and even owned exactly the same lilac T-shirt from *New Look* – Sophy's aunt had sent hers from the mainland and she wore it all the time. It was simply weird to think how alike they were – especially considering that Sophy lived on a remote Scottish island and Kate came from a Lancashire mill town hundreds of miles away.

Sophy tried to concentrate on the postcard she was writing to her mum and dad. None of the contestants were allowed to speak to their families, so even though she *hated* writing, this was the only way of keeping in touch. It was strictly against the rules but she was pretty sure that Scooter had smuggled a mobile phone into the academy. She suspected Astoria had too.

'It's *very busy here,*' Sophy had written. '*We've been singing and dancing all day. I think I'm singing first this Saturday. Don't forget to watch. Love you lots…*'

Suddenly the door of the girls' dorm swung open and Astoria struggled in, weighed down with bags. She was wearing blue flowery pyjamas and had loads of tiny purple rollers in her hair.

'I thought you might like a bit of company,' said Astoria in a matter-of-fact sort of voice. 'Now that Kate's gone, I mean.'

Sophy stared at her, trying to take in this unexpected announcement. Astoria hadn't said anything about changing rooms before. She'd always made it perfectly plain she wanted to be by herself.

'Well don't nick Kate's bed. It wouldn't be fair because she'll be back soon.'

Astoria looked startled. According to Didi, Kate had quit the contest for good.

'What makes you say that? She seemed in a pretty bad way in the ambulance.'

Sophy shrugged her shoulders obstinately.

'Dunno. But I know she will. She's a determined sort of lass. She won't give up without a fight.'

'Well, that's not what Didi told me,' said Astoria, a sly expression crossing her face.

Sophy put down her pen and glared at Astoria.

'What? What did Didi tell you? When were you talking to her? The rest of us haven't set eyes on her all week. Me

148

and Scooter thought she and Zaza must be too busy swanning around that swanky hotel of theirs.'

Astoria's face flushed bright red. Why on earth had she gone and opened her big mouth?

'Oh, I just bumped into her downstairs earlier on,' said Astoria casually. 'We had a quick chat. She didn't say anything much — just talked about the weather and things. But she didn't think Kate would come back.'

Sophy stared intently at Astoria. It was obvious she was lying. Her body language was all wrong. She kept shifting from one foot to the other and wouldn't look her in the eye properly.

'Well, Didi's completely off her trolley,' declared Sophy. 'Kate'll be back. You wait and see.'

Astoria didn't feel quite so pleased with herself the next morning when she rushed into breakfast forty minutes late, trailing her dance gear on the floor and with her hair still in curlers.

'You might have woken me up,' she yelled at Sophy, who was calmly tucking into a bowl of muesli and chatting away to Tommy about her little brother's antics.

'That's a bit rich coming from you,' snapped Sophy. 'The alarm went off at seven-thirty and I came over and shook you awake about three times. Honestly Astoria, you gave me so much grief that I stopped trying in the end.'

Astoria didn't reply, just stuck out her bottom lip crossly.

Scooter leaned across the table and whispered furtively to Sophy.

'D'you know who she reminds me of when she does that?'

'Who?' grinned Sophy.

'Violet Elizabeth Bott. You know, the girl in the *Just*

William books. The one who says *"I'll scweam and scweam and scweam until I make myself sick."* Have you read them?'

Sophy and Tommy burst out laughing at this. Tears began to stream down their faces and soon they were unable to string two words together. When Scooter started addressing Astoria as 'Vi' they became even more incoherent.

'I don't know what you think is so funny,' said Astoria coldly. Honestly. Why were they so juvenile? They were even sillier than the Kidstars lot – and that was saying something. She stalked over to the side table and helped herself to a bowl of porridge and a glass of orange juice. Dottie had kept hammering home the importance of eating a proper breakfast and the message had finally begun to sink in.

Astoria pointedly carried her breakfast to the other end of the table and sat as far away from the others as possible. Someone had left a couple of morning newspapers lying around and she grabbed one of them to read.

She took a mouthful of steaming hot porridge and spluttered with shock.

'I don't believe it,' she gasped. 'I don't blinking well believe it. It's not fair. It's just not fair. Have the rest of you seen this?'

Sophy and Tommy carried on chatting, while Scooter had picked up his GameBoy.

'I say,' shrieked Astoria at the top of her voice. 'Kate's only gone and made it on to the front page again. It's not fair. It's just not.'

At the mention of Kate's name, Sophy and Tommy broke off their conversation and came and peered over Astoria's shoulder.

'Blooming Nora,' muttered Sophy, copying Dottie's favourite catchphrase. 'How on earth did that happen? Daniel Drewsome will go completely potty when he sees it.'

'Too right he will,' said Tommy, pole-axed by the enormous headline on the front page of the *Daily Despatch*.

'*STARSPOTTER GIRL FIGHTS FOR LIFE IN BOATING DISASTER*,' said Sophy, reading aloud.

'Well that's a load of garbage for a start,' said Tommy. 'She's absolutely fine.'

Sophy continued to read from the *Daily Despatch*.

'*Singer Kate Barnsley almost died when she fell into an icy lake while filming for the children's breakfast TV show* Rise and Shine. *Kate, 13, who has been tipped to win the show's popular Starspotter competition …*'

Astoria was incensed by this.

'That's rubbish,' she said. 'How can they say that? We've only been here for a week and no one has a clue *who's* going to win. And anyway, Kate's not even in the competition any more…'

But Sophy was still gripped by the *Daily Despatch* story.

'*… If it hadn't been for the quick thinking of boatman Ned Lister and fellow competitor Tommy Brown, 13, Kate might have drowned …* Hey Tommy, that's you. You're famous.'

'It's a slight exaggeration,' said Tommy bashfully. 'You must admit. I mean, she was wearing a life jacket, wasn't she? And she must be able to swim a few strokes, surely?'

Sophy elbowed him in the ribs playfully.

'Don't be so modest. You and Ned saved her. You know you did. It's about time someone said so.'

Tommy blushed, embarrassed at the fuss, and tried to change the subject.

'I wonder how the paper found out about it,' he said. 'I mean, Daniel Drewsome was trying to hush it up. In case it made *Rise and Shine* sound irresponsible and stuff. What d'you reckon, Scooter?'

Up till now Scooter had stayed glued to his GameBoy, not saying a word. This was highly unusual. He was generally the first to leap in when something was afoot.

'You what?' mumbled Scooter, not even bothering to look up. 'Oh look, can't you sort it out for yourselves. I'm on the verge of making it to the next level.'

Sophy stared at Scooter in amazement. She'd only known him for a week but he was behaving very oddly. Very oddly indeed.

And then, all of a sudden, everything fell into place. Scooter's habit of disappearing by himself at night. Her hunch that he'd brought a mobile phone with him to the Starspotter Academy. His studied indifference now.

'What paper was it you said your dad works for, Scooter?' she asked in a casual sort of voice.

Startled, Scooter looked up from his game.

'You what?'

'You heard,' said Sophy firmly. 'You told us your dad's a reporter. Which paper does he work for then?'

'It's not one you'll have heard of,' mumbled Scooter.

'Try me,' said Sophy.

Tommy glanced at her in bewilderment. He'd never seen Sophy in this kind of mood before.

'The *Slough Sentinel*,' Scooter muttered quickly.

Sophy stomped across to where Scooter was sitting. She placed her finger under his chin and forced him to look up.

'You're fibbing. You said it was a national paper, not a local one.'

At this, Scooter completely lost his temper. He slammed his GameBoy on the table and jumped to his feet.

'OK, Sherlock Holmes,' he shouted, jabbing his finger at Sophy. 'He works for the *Daily Despatch*. And so what? I spoke to him on my mobile yesterday – and yes Miss Goody Two-Shoes, I know that's against the rules too. And yes, I just happened to mention to him that Kate had fallen into the lake but I never dreamed he'd tell the paper about it. So yes, you're right on all counts. I've been a complete prize idiot. Are you satisfied?'

Scooter grabbed his GameBoy and stormed out of the room, slamming the door behind him as he went.

'Oh dear,' said Sophy. 'What are we going to do now?'

18
Scooter in a Sulk

EVERYONE WAS in a foul mood that day. First Sean, the normally genial chief cameraman, shouted at Sophy for tripping over his gear in the hall. When Astoria tried to interrogate Dottie about the story in the *Daily Despatch*, Dottie curtly told her to 'mind your own business.' And when Scooter failed to show up for GG's class at nine a.m. the hot-tempered dance teacher completely lost her rag and ordered Tommy to fetch him.

'I don't care what's wrong with the boy,' she screeched at Tommy. 'Even if he's got a splitting headache … Even if he's broken his ankle … Even if he's … Oh just go and get him, will you? I want him down here in five minutes flat. Or he won't know he's born.'

Tommy scurried out of the ballroom. Oh dear. He didn't know what this place was coming to. The last time he'd had to cope with dramas on this scale was when Sinead and Scarlett, his twin sisters, had started going out with boys. He'd give anything to be back on the football pitch with his pals from *Grove Park Wanderers*. They had their heads screwed on all right. None of them got in such a stew about things. He felt completed exhausted with all this drama.

Tommy pushed open the door of the boys' dorm and crept in. Scooter was standing by the window, gazing out over Lake Valewater. He was talking to someone on his mobile.

'How could you do it, Dad? How could you? I never

realised you'd use all that stuff I told you. I'm in real trouble now. Deep trouble. They're probably going to throw me out for this.'

Sensing someone behind him, Scooter whirled round to see who it was.

'What's that, Dad? Oh, yeah, sure. But I've got to go now. No, I probably won't be able to ring till the weekend. And no. No. No. Of course I can't tip you off on what else is happening. How can you ask such a thing?'

Scooter's face darkened as he switched off his phone and stuffed it in his pocket.

'Your dad?' asked Tommy, well aware he was stating the obvious.

Scooter nodded wearily.

'Yeah.'

'Sounds like you gave him what-for.'

'Yeah,' said Scooter once more.

Tommy opened his mouth to say something, then shut it again.

'You look like a goldfish when you do that,' observed Scooter.

Tommy stared at him.

'When I do what?'

'When you open and close your mouth. That's what my brother's goldfish does. He's called Goldie.'

Tommy burst out laughing.

'That's the first time I've ever been compared to a goldfish,' he chuckled. 'Honestly, Scooter, you're a plonker. You're in real trouble. Your brother's goldfish is the last thing you should be thinking about.'

Scooter gazed down at his trainers. He was very proud of them. They were white with silver stripes – the very height of trainer fashion. His dad was very generous when it came to trainers.

'I didn't mean it to happen, you know,' he said. 'I just

155

liked chatting to my dad. I never thought he'd go and pull a stunt like this. I mean, I only mentioned it in passing. I never dreamed he'd use it in the paper.'

'I know, mate. I know. And if you play your cards right maybe no one will find out. We've all had a chat downstairs and agreed not to tell on you. But you should get rid of that mobile of yours. In double quick time if I were you.'

Scooter looked panic-stricken.

'I can't do that. It cost a fortune. My dad will go mad with me.'

Tommy looked thoughtful.

'I know,' he said. 'I've got a better idea. Quick, give it here.'

Scooter reluctantly handed the tiny phone over, then watched in puzzlement as Tommy walked towards the door, knelt down on the wooden floor and started knocking the floorboards.

'Now who's gone loopy in the head?' said Scooter, bewildered by his friend's actions. 'What are you doing?'

'Aah, here it is,' said Tommy. With his fingertips he expertly levered up one of the floorboards and felt inside the gap. Then he dropped the phone into the hole and replaced the floorboard.

'Looks good as new, doesn't it? I spotted that one of the boards was loose the other day. Don't worry, it'll be safe there. No one will ever think of looking for it under the floorboards. Now come on, we'd better get back to GG's class. She's spitting pins as it is.'

Over at the Brackenside Hotel, Daniel Drewsome and Dottie were deep in conversation.

Dottie's heart had plummeted when she spotted the front page of the *Daily Despatch* first thing. She was so alarmed by how Daniel would react that she hadn't bothered to wonder *who* had tipped the newspaper off.

But Daniel had. He'd cancelled the Starspotter lesson on interview techniques and summoned Dottie to the Brackenside Hotel.

'None of us have breathed a word,' he yelled, banging his fist on the white wrought iron table. 'How could this happen? How did it get out?'

Dottie and Daniel were sitting on the hotel's sunny terrace. A waitress in a formal black dress and white apron had hurried out with coffee for Dottie and hot water for Daniel. Both sat untouched on the table.

Dottie opened her mouth to express her opinion. But with Daniel in this mood it was impossible to get a word in edgeways.

'Perhaps we should think of a way of …' she began.

'We need to do something,' raged Daniel, interrupting her again. 'And do it fast.'

Dottie tried once again.

'I'm sure that our best strategy would be to …'

Daniel banged on the table once more. He hit the surface so hard that the bone china cups rattled on their saucers.

'Got it,' he shouted.

Dottie wished Daniel would keep his voice down. The elderly couple sipping coffee at the next table kept glancing nervously at him. The Brackenside, set halfway up the fell, was renowned for its tranquillity, haute cuisine and mind-boggling prices. Daniel Drewsome, with his shades, long hair, black jeans and white T-shirt with the words *Hell's Angel* emblazoned across it, didn't fit in at all.

'What?' asked Dottie nervously. She knew that whatever Daniel decided was bound to involve her. Delegating things he didn't want to do himself – that was the way he worked.

'We have to make people realise that Kate's accident wasn't serious at all. It was just a silly prank really, wasn't it? A load of kids having fun on the lake. Perfectly normal. Happens all the time.'

'Er, no,' said the ever-honest Dottie. 'It wasn't a prank at all, Daniel. You know it wasn't. I really thought Kate might …'

But Daniel, as per usual, didn't take a blind bit of notice.

'Good, Dottie. Good. I knew we were on the same wavelength. Now, what we need to do is this. You'll have to go down to – where is it the wretched girl lives again?'

'Gribblesdale,' said Dottie, doing her best to stay calm. There was no point arguing with Daniel when he was in this mood.

'That's it. Gribblesdale. Yep. Right. Get straight down there and tell Kate she's back in the competition. Take Garcia with you and then all of you check into a hotel near Penrith. Not too far away. Get Garcia to give the girl some coaching tomorrow and then hey presto, she can join the finalists on Saturday. We'll put her on last and she'll show everyone she's as right as rain and, yep, everything will be fine and dandy. It'll make smashing telly …'

Daniel was getting carried away with the ingenuity of his idea now, talking at the top of his voice and waving his arms around in excitement.

Dottie wasn't impressed.

'Can I just mention one thing, Daniel?' she said. 'Something you seem to have forgotten.'

Daniel gazed out towards Lake Valewater. This view was all right, he supposed, but give him Notting Hill any day, with its noisy hubbub, cool shops and swanky cars and nightclubs.

'What's that?' he murmured absent-mindedly, still staring into the distance.

'What if Kate's mum won't let her come back? What if

Linda Barnsley puts her foot down and says we can get stuffed? What then?'

Daniel's face prickled with irritation.

'You what?' he said. 'Oh don't be so negative, Dottie. You know it'll work. Just get it sorted, will you? The mum can come too if she likes. Have a bit of a jaunt. Oh, and keep it under your hat. Don't breathe a word to anyone apart from Garcia. We can trust him.'

19
Kate Gets a Shock

KATE WAS fed up and bored. Her mum had managed to wangle three days off work to look after her but now it was Thursday and she had to go back to the factory.

'I'm sorry about this, sweetheart,' Linda told Kate when she came into her bedroom at seven-thirty to say goodbye. 'The personnel woman at Brydale's says they're really short-staffed. I'm desperate to stay with you but I haven't got any choice. I can't afford to get on the wrong side of them.'

'It's OK, Mum,' said Kate, trying to force a smile. 'I'll be fine. Really I will.'

Linda Barnsley looked intently at her daughter. The colour had returned to her cheeks and she *did* look an awful lot better. Virtually back to normal really. But she still hated leaving her.

'You will stay indoors, won't you? And don't open the door to anyone. D'you promise me?'

'You don't need to worry so much,' grinned Kate. 'I *am* thirteen, you know.'

'Promise me?' repeated Linda. 'I won't take no for any answer.'

'I promise.'

Things wouldn't be quite so bad, thought Kate once the front door slammed, if Sally was around. Sally was her best friend from school. She lived in the next street and, come rain or shine, the two of them cycled to school together every morning. Only Sally was on a caravanning holiday in Scarborough with her family this week and Kate wasn't in the mood to see anyone else. She couldn't face their nosy questions about why she was back home all of a sudden and what had gone wrong.

It was well after noon by the time Kate woke again. She stretched her arms above her head and yawned lazily. Why was she so tired all the time? She'd been sleeping for fifteen hours a day since she got home. She padded downstairs in her pyjamas, made herself a brew and then ambled into the front room to switch on the telly. Watching TV was just about the only thing she fancied doing.

As the telly flickered to life, an instantly recognisable face appeared on the screen. Kate stopped plucking more stray threads from the sofa and stared at it in disbelief. It was her. It was a clip of her from last week's *Rise and Shine*, singing the duet with Garcia. Why on earth were they using that now?

After a few bars, the music died away and a blonde-haired newsreader in a jade green jacket popped up onscreen.

'That was the young singer Kate Barnsley, one of the Starspotter contestants from the children's TV show *Rise and Shine*,' announced the newsreader. 'The show has denied allegations that 13-year-old Kate nearly drowned this week when a boating trip went tragically wrong.'

Kate put her hands to her face in horror. She could hardly bear to watch. It was weird to think that out of the blue her stupid accident on the lake had turned into a national news story.

'A report in today's *Daily Despatch* newspaper has claimed that Kate, who comes from Gribblesdale in Lancashire, fell into Lake Valewater on Sunday,' continued the newsreader. 'The newspaper alleges she was admitted to hospital suffering from shock and hypo-thermia and has had to leave the competition as a result of the trauma.

'But a spokesman for *Rise and Shine* has insisted that the incident was just a silly teenage prank. He said Kate was absolutely fine and would be appearing on the show as usual on Saturday morning. We hope to be able to get the full story from Kate herself before the end of this lunchtime news bulletin ...'

Kate sat motionless for several minutes as she tried to get her head round what she had just heard. None of it made sense. For a start, why had *Rise and Shine* said she would be appearing on the show on Saturday when in fact she was sitting at home in Gribblesdale twiddling her thumbs? And what did the newsreader mean by the ominous words 'we hope to get the full story from Kate herself...?'

Glancing idly out of the front room window, Kate got the answer to her second question. A crowd of people were standing in the middle of Bright Street, gazing across at number 14. Compared to the inhabitants of Gribblesdale, they looked like exotic creatures from another planet. Most of them were smartly dressed and talking intently into mobile phones. Boxes, bags and mounds of camera gear were strewn on the ground all around them.

'What the blazes is going on?' Kate muttered to herself. She got up from the sofa and moved to the side of the window to get a better look.

At that moment a young woman in a sharply cut navy trouser suit snapped her mobile shut and strode across the road. A balding, middle-aged man with a flash-looking camera slung round his neck accompanied her. Seconds later there was a sharp rap at the door.

Kate moved like lightning. Frightened out of her wits,

she dived to the floor. Her mum had told her not to answer the door to anyone and she had no intention of disobeying her instructions, especially with this army of strangers assembled outside. And especially when she was wearing her scruffiest, oldest pyjamas and her hair looked as if she'd been pulled through a hedge backwards.

But when Kate glanced back at the telly she was in for an even greater shock. A man in a dark blue jacket was onscreen now, standing against a backdrop of redbrick terraced houses. He spoke earnestly to the camera.

'Oh no,' gasped Kate. 'That's Bright Street ...'

'... We're broadcasting live this lunchtime from the small town in Lancashire where Kate Barnsley lives. We're not sure if the youngster is at home or not but let's go and find out ...'

Kate switched off the telly, then slithered across the floor on her stomach. When she made it into the hallway, she fled up the stairs, gasping for breath. Her room was at the front of the house, overlooking the street, so she rushed into Linda's bedroom and collapsed panic-stricken on to the bed.

She felt like a cornered animal. She was completely trapped – her mum wouldn't be back from work till late afternoon and she couldn't even ring for help because the phone was still disconnected.

Her mind racing, Kate crawled under Linda's flowery duvet and began to cry. She'd never felt so alone.

Dottie experienced a rising sense of foreboding. She and Garcia had been negotiating the back streets of Gribblesdale in their rented Fiat for twenty minutes now and despite asking several people for directions, they still hadn't found Bright Street. If they didn't get there soon, Kate would be nobbled by a load of reporters. Maybe they'd interviewed her already.

As they drove down one identical terraced street after another, Dottie was shocked to see how rundown Gribblesdale was. She remembered the way Kate and Linda had burst out laughing at the audition when she'd asked them if it was a nice place to live. Nice was certainly not the word to describe it, thought Dottie. There was graffiti scrawled across every wall and, she wrinkled her nose with distaste, a horrible smell of rotten eggs in the air. It seemed a different world to London or Manchester.

At that moment Dottie spotted a boy doing wheelies on his bike and wound down the car window.

'Can you tell us how to get to Bright Street?' she yelled.

'What's it worth, doll?' The boy was about fourteen, wiry and thin, with bright blue eyes and a cheeky expression.

'What d'you mean "what's it worth?"'

'Keep your hair on, missus. I were only joking. Can't you take a joke?'

Dottie chuckled despite herself.

'Course I can. It's just that we're in a bit of a hurry to get to Bright Street. D'you know it?'

'Course I do,' said the boy. 'It's two streets from here. Only there's a bit of a jam at the moment. Dunno why but there's loads of telly cameras and reporters milling about.'

'Why's that?' said Dottie. She kept her voice casual but she had a blooming good idea why. Daniel had been on the phone to her and Garcia non-stop during the two-hour drive from the Lake District, droning on and on about the stream of idiotic press inquiries he was getting about Kate.

'Dunno.'

Dottie thought quickly. If she and Garcia were going to talk to Kate and her mum, the last thing in the world they needed was a gang of reporters swarming around.

'Listen,' she told the boy. 'What did you say your name was?'

164

'I didn't. But since you're asking, it's Danny. Danny Shaw.'

'OK Danny,' said Dottie. 'Look, I'll be straight with you. We're from the TV show *Rise and Shine* and we need to get into a house in Bright Street without anyone seeing. Can you help us out? There's a couple of *Rise and Shine* tickets in it for you if you can. '

Kate had no idea how long she'd been lying under her mum's duvet. She'd lost count of the number of times people had knocked on the door once it got to twenty. She just wished that her mum would hurry up and get home from her shift. She'd know what to do.

Suddenly there was a strange clink against the window. Her heart started to beat wildly again. What was that? Oh no. The reporters must have come round the back. Her mum was always forgetting to lock the gate. But surely they wouldn't break into the house? They wouldn't do that. Would they?

Kate got out of bed and tiptoed slowly to the bedroom window. As she pressed her nose to the glass, a pebble hit the windowpane, making her jump back with fright. She peered forward again nervously and … her eyes nearly popped out of her head. Standing in the tiny back yard they shared with next-door, was the unmistakable figure of Garcia Andrew. And behind him, scrabbling around on the ground for another stone to chuck, was Dottie. A solitary tear ran down Kate's cheek. She'd never been so pleased to see anyone in her entire life.

'Cor, this is like something out of a film,' grinned Kate as Garcia and Dottie hurried her through the cobbled back yard, past bins overflowing with rubbish and into the grotty-looking alleyway that ran behind all the houses in Bright Street. None of the reporters had twigged there was a back entrance, so the three of them were able to scuttle to the car unseen by anyone. Apart from Danny, that is, who stood guard at the end of the alleyway. The boy winked at them conspiratorially, gave Dottie a cheery thumbs-up and cycled off down the street.

Much to her embarrassment Kate was still wearing the tatty old pyjamas she'd slept in. She'd been desperate to get dressed but Dottie insisted there was no time to lose. All she could do was hurriedly fling on a sweatshirt and grab her trainers.

'We need you back in Cumbria double-quick,' said Dottie, gabbling her words as she started the car. 'Daniel wants you in the show for Saturday's grand finale. But we have to get your mum's permission first. She won't have left work yet, will she?'

Kate glanced at the digital clock on the dashboard. It said 15:15.

'No. She doesn't finish till four. Eight till four – that's her usual shift. Apart from when she's on nights, that is.'

'So who looks after you when she's on nights?' asked Dottie.

'Mrs Tate from next door used to come round when I was younger. But now I manage by myself. Mum doesn't like leaving me – she says she'd be in real trouble if anyone found out I was on my own – but she can't afford a sitter.'

Dottie glanced at Kate in her rear view mirror. This kid had it tougher than most, she thought. She deserved a break.

Brydale's, the textiles factory where Linda Barnsley worked, was only a mile or so from Bright Street. In winter Linda caught the bus. In summer, she either walked or borrowed Kate's bike.

The car drew up outside a massive redbrick building. It reminded Dottie more of a prison than a factory. Some of the windows on the upper storeys had been smashed and it was bordered by a tatty barbed wire fence.

'Is this it?' said Dottie.

'Yep,' said Kate. She did a pretend fanfare. 'De-da-de-da. Welcome to Brydale's. The most famous school uniform factory in the world.'

'What's with the barbed wire?'

Kate shrugged her shoulders with disinterest.

'Not sure. Vandalism, I think. My mum has to show a special pass to get in.'

'How long has your mum worked here?'

'Ever since Dad left,' answered Kate. 'She always stayed at home to look after me when I was little, but once he'd gone she didn't really have any choice. And she's brilliant at sewing.'

'Is that what she does here?' asked Garcia.

'Yep. They make shirts, trousers, skirts, that sort of thing. Mum can churn them out in her sleep.'

It was only when they got out of the car that Kate remembered she was still wearing her pyjamas.

'Please Dottie, I can't go in like this,' she pleaded. 'They're a real rowdy lot in there ... honestly, I'd never live it down. And nor would Mum. Can you go in without me?'

Dottie was on the verge of telling Kate to pull herself together when she spotted the mortified expression on the youngster's face. Flummoxed, she glanced down at her own outfit for inspiration. Suddenly an idea came to her.

Dottie was never one to follow the crowd when it came to fashion. Today she was wearing a denim mini skirt over a pair of red and white striped leggings and red clogs that clip-clopped as she walked. She quickly unfastened the mini skirt and handed it to Kate.

'Put this on,' she instructed. 'Look. It matches your

167

sweatshirt. And *you've* got the legs to carry it off. I wish I had legs as long as yours.'

The unlikely-looking trio traipsed across the car park to a small hut marked 'Reception. All visitors report here.' Inside, a bored-looking man in a navy blue uniform and peaked cap sat with his feet up on the desk. He was sipping beer from a can and watching snooker on a tiny TV.

He quickly stuffed the beer can under the desk as they entered.

'What d'you lot want?' he mumbled, his eyes flicking back to the snooker.

Dottie nodded to Kate to do the talking.

'It … it's an emergency,' spluttered Kate. 'My mum works here … on the factory floor … And I need to see her. I need to see her this minute.'

'Do you now?' said the man, still keeping his eyes fixed to the TV.

His lethargic response infuriated Dottie.

'Did you hear what she just said?' she yelled. 'Or are you deaf as well as stupid? She needs to see her mum. It's important.'

The man looked up and glared at Dottie.

'Well, that's tough, love – because you'll just have to wait till the snooker's finished. And there's quite a few more frames to go yet.'

Seething with anger, Dottie shifted her weight from one foot to the other. They were forty-eight hours away from the Starspotter final. The sooner they whisked Kate back up to the Lake District and got her into rehearsals the better. The other finalists had had four more days than her to practise and Dottie couldn't bear it if Kate made a fool of herself. The embarrassment of walking through Gribblesdale in her pyjamas would be nothing compared to messing up on live TV.

Garcia had remained silent, happy to let Kate and

168

Dottie to do the talking. But now the singer wasn't prepared to put up with the man's surliness a minute longer.

'Who's winning?' he asked in his rich, velvety voice.

'Stephen Hendry,' said the man. He glanced up to see who was speaking and did a double take. The tall man in a flamboyant burgundy corduroy suit looked awfully familiar. ''Ere, don't I recognise you?'

'Maybe,' said Garcia. 'But ...'

'Hey, I know who you are ...'

The man got up from his chair and walked round his desk to take a closer look. Garcia towered over him.

'You're Garcia Andrew, you are,' said the man, beaming with self-importance. 'My wife's got all your records. Nuts about you, she is. I couldn't have your autograph for her, could I? She'd be made up with it.'

Dottie grinned in spite of herself. This was a bit of a turn up for the books. One moment this man was treating the three of them like nobodies, the next he was grovelling around asking for Garcia's autograph.

'Possibly,' said Garcia. 'But on one condition.'

'What's that?' said the man quickly.

'That before I do ... what did you say your name was?'

'Bill,' said the man. 'Bill Potts. And the wife's Elsie.'

'Right Bill,' said Garcia. 'Listen to me. This is the deal. You take us straight in to see Linda Barnsley, no messing, and I'll give Elsie her autograph.'

After this exchange, Bill Potts turned into a different person. Mustering every ounce of charm he possessed – which admittedly wasn't bucket loads – he led them up a short flight of steps to the factory floor.

Dottie gasped when she saw it. The room was the size of an aircraft hangar, with box-sized offices down one side and rows and rows of workers, mainly women, bent over sewing machines down the other. She put her hands over

169

her ears to block out the din. The noise of the machines going nineteen to the dozen was terrible.

Bill Potts marched up to the assembly line supervisor, a middle-aged woman in a pink overall, who was busy patrolling the floor.

'This young lady needs to see Linda Barnsley, Brenda,' he said. 'Can you sort it?'

But before the supervisor could reply Linda herself came flying down the central aisle in a mad panic. She looked so shocked to see Kate standing in the middle of the factory floor that she didn't even clock Garcia Andrew's presence at all.

'Kate love, Kate love,' she shrieked.

Instantly every sewing machine in the place ceased whirring as everyone looked up to see what the commotion was.

'I told you not to leave the house. What are you doing here? Has something happened? Quick love, tell me.'

20
The Safe House

DOTTIE WAS so anxious that the reporters might get wind of what they were up to that she refused point-blank to let Kate and Linda fetch their belongings from Bright Street.

'This is all a bit cloak and dagger, isn't it?' protested Garcia.

'Tell me about it,' sighed Dottie. A wave of guilt swept over her. 'But we can't be too careful. Daniel reckons that if we keep Kate out of sight till Saturday, the viewing figures will go through the roof. He says the whole country will be on tenterhooks watching *Rise and Shine* to find out whether she's going to appear or not.'

Linda didn't like the sound of this at all. She'd agreed, against her better judgement, to let Kate return for the final show – but only on the strict condition that she came too.

Uppermost in Kate's mind, however, was the worry that she didn't have any decent clothes with her.

'What will me and Mum wear?' asked Kate. 'I've only got my pyjamas and your skirt, Dottie. I can't keep wearing them, can I? And poor Mum's in her work overall.'

'And very fetching it is too,' beamed Garcia, glancing over the back seat.

Linda smiled wanly. She couldn't believe she'd agreed to this stunt. She must have taken leave of her senses.

But Dottie had everything figured out.

'Don't worry, you two,' said Dottie, trying to concentrate on the motorway traffic. It was the beginning of the rush hour and the M6 was heaving with cars. 'I know it's a pain for you but there's a hypermarket near Kendal that stays open late. We'll stop off and get everything you need. Clothes, shoes, toothpaste, the works. All on *Rise and Shine* of course. Is that OK with you, Linda?'

'We haven't got much choice, have we?' said Linda, her voice gruff.

Kate squeezed her mum's hand to cheer her up.

'That's great,' she said. 'We could do with some new outfits.'

The SaverStore hypermarket came up trumps for both of them. Kate was thrilled with her new jeans, vests and leotards and could hardly believe it when Dottie insisted she fling two pairs of trainers and some pink pumps into the trolley too. Even Linda had to admit – albeit grudgingly – that her stuff was a bit of all right.

After tea and sandwiches in the SaverStore Café, Dottie and Garcia swapped seats once more. They'd shared the driving all the way and now it was Garcia's turn again.

'Where is it that we're heading?' he asked Dottie.

'It's a small private hotel in a village the other side of Penrith,' says Dottie. 'In the Eden Valley. The people who own the Brackenside told Daniel about it. It's only got five rooms and I've booked all of them – so it should be top notch.'

It was dark when Garcia turned the car into the drive of the Moorlands Inn.

'They said they'd leave some supper for us,' Dottie told Kate and Linda. 'It's really important that you look after yourself properly, Kate. You've had quite a time of it – and the next two days will be mad.'

The Moorlands Inn turned out to be the perfect retreat. A mile from the nearest village, it perched high on a hill looking towards the Lakeland fells and was run by a husband-and-wife team called Robin and Sally Burford. Robin did all the cooking while Sally took charge of everything else. The instant Garcia drew up outside the hotel's pretty, rose-clad porch, the pair came rushing out to greet them.

'Good journey, I trust?' said Robin, who was still wearing his chef's whites. 'I'll bring your luggage in.'

Robin didn't bat an eyelid when he saw that the luggage consisted of a vast number of fluorescent yellow carrier bags from the Kendal branch of SaverStore.

'Er, we forgot a few bits and pieces so we had to buy some stuff on the way up,' said Dottie, trying to explain.

'What a good idea,' said Robin amiably. 'I hate packing too.'

After a delicious supper of poached salmon, new potatoes and green salad, Linda told Kate it was high time she got some sleep. Once they'd disappeared upstairs, Sally took Dottie and Garcia to one side.

'There's something I want to show you,' she said, leading them down a long passageway and into the garden.

'Where on earth are we going?' asked Dottie. 'This is a bit cloak and dagger, isn't it?'

'Wait and see,' said Sally. 'I think you'll be pleased.'

The hotelier walked down the garden path and towards a low, square building at the far side of the lawn.

'You two go in first,' said Sally. 'The light switch is on the left by the way. I want to see what you think.'

Dottie went first. She pushed open the door and fumbled for the switch. She snapped it on and suddenly the building lit up like a beacon.

'It's fantastic,' said Dottie, blinking at the dazzlingly bright lights. 'A dance studio. This is the last thing I expected. It's just right.'

Following close behind, Sally Burford beamed with pleasure.

'The people who owned the hotel before us used to run a dance school here,' she explained. 'We only use it for parties now but Kate will be able to rehearse in complete privacy. And look at this ...'

Sally pointed to a pile of audio equipment in the corner.

'... Mr Drewsome arranged for this to be sent over earlier on. He's written reams of instructions about what to rehearse. All top secret, of course. I promise I haven't peeked.'

Excitement was written all over Dottie's face. All of a sudden everything seemed possible.

'Kate will really be able to get up to speed with her performance here. Don't you think, Garcia?'

The singer grinned at Dottie.

'Sure,' he said. 'She'll be singing and dancing like Madonna by Saturday morning.'

The next day started off badly. When Kate came down to breakfast, she was devastated to find that Dottie had disappeared back to the Starspotter Academy at dawn to supervise the other finalists.

'I'm really sorry, Kate, but she has to give them some support too,' Garcia told Kate. 'Astoria's OK, but Sophy, Scooter and Tommy have really taken their eyes off the ball since you went home. Dottie needs to check they're back on track.'

Kate had barely sung a note for four days, so being plunged into a series of intensive singing lessons with Garcia was tough. Watching Garcia put her through her paces, Linda had to force herself not to protest at how hard the singer was working her daughter.

At four p.m., just as Linda thought Kate should be

packing up for the day, Dottie returned with an unexpected visitor in tow.

Kate groaned. It was GG.

The dance teacher looked scarier than ever. Kate had forgotten how scarlet her lipstick was and how deathly-white her complexion. Typically, GG barely bothered to greet everyone. She placed her posh leather bag on the ground – 'There's a six-month waiting list for one of those,' Garcia whispered to Linda – and climbed out of her chic black tracksuit. Then, clad in her customary black leotard and leggings, it was down to work.

'I hope you've been doing your exercises everyday, Kate,' said GG, limbering up.

Kate stared at her. She didn't dare to admit that she'd been lying in bed till lunchtime and watching telly all afternoon.

'Er yes, GG,' she said, lying through her teeth. 'Of course I have. Everyday.'

The next two hours were probably the most gruelling Kate had ever experienced. After a short warm-up, GG made Kate go over her moves again and again, practising till they were perfect. Or as near as possible.

Finally, she switched off the music and put her tracksuit back on. She even did that elegantly, thought Kate.

'That's all I can do with you, Kate,' said GG briskly. 'We'll just have to see how you get on tomorrow. Do your very best, won't you?'

21
The Final Countdown

ASTORIA OPENED one eye lazily, then closed it tight shut again. The clock by her bedside said six a.m. but it felt more like the middle of the night.

She was about to snuggle down again when it dawned on her what day it was. It was Saturday – the day of the Starspotter final.

Astoria stumbled out of bed, her heart hammering with excitement. She stalked straight across to Sophy's bed and pulled her friend's duvet off with a flourish.

'Hey, w...what are you doing?' protested Sophy, trying to grab it back.

'Quick, lazybones, get up,' hissed Astoria. 'Quick. It's *Rise and Shine* day, silly. We have to be with the wardrobe girls by six forty-five. And in make-up by seven-fifteen. Come on. We need to get going.'

Just like the week before, *Rise and Shine*'s wardrobe department had set up a temporary changing room in an office on the ground floor of the Starspotter Academy. A quarter of it had been screened off for Tommy and Scooter while Didi, Zaza, Sophy and Astoria got the remainder. Didi had kicked up a stink about not having a dressing room to herself but the team had ignored her. Everyone was fed up with her demands.

Sue and Charlotte, the two wardrobe girls, had arrived at the academy on Thursday, bringing with them a lorry-load of outfits of every imaginable colour and design. Typically, Didi had managed to sneak in before anyone else – just to make doubly sure that hers would be the most spectacular outfit. She'd also tipped Astoria the wink, telling her to nab a fabulous pair of sparkly turquoise hot-pants and a matching top.

Over the past few days, Didi had kept her promise about helping Astoria. The TV presenter had advised her which song to perform at the finale – 'You need a real showstopper…' she'd instructed. She'd coached her on how to charm the viewers at home – 'Eyes and teeth, darling, eyes and teeth.' She'd also cautioned Astoria against appearing too arrogant and full of herself. 'Make sure you come across as sweet and modest – just like me,' Didi had told her. 'And when I ask you who are your most important influences, don't for goodness sake say Christina Aguilera and Britney Spears. Say your mum and dad. That always goes down well.'

'Are you nervous?' Sophy asked Astoria as they hurried downstairs to breakfast.

'No, of course not. Why? Are you?'

Sophy stared at Astoria, astonished.

'How can you *not* be nervous? We're going to have millions of people watching our every move in a couple of hours' time.'

In truth, Astoria felt scared stiff. But she wasn't going to show it. Certainly not to Sophy. No way. They were deadly rivals now.

Over at the Moorlands Inn, Garcia and Linda were doing their best to bolster Kate's dwindling morale. Robin Burford had decided to serve breakfast in the kitchen for a change, so conversation was interspersed with the sound of clashing saucepans and Robin frying bacon on the massive industrial cooker.

'A good breakfast,' said Robin, plonking a plate of bacon and eggs in front of a pale-looking Kate. 'That's what you need. You've got a big day ahead. This'll build up your strength.'

'That's what Dottie's always saying,' smiled Kate. 'But I'm not sure I can …'

'Get it eaten, love,' Linda ordered her daughter. 'We're not having you passing out with hunger halfway through the show. Come on, it'll do you a power of good.'

At seven, Ken, the minibus driver, arrived in a shiny yellow souped-up Mini Cooper with blacked-out windows, ready to drive Kate and Linda to the Starspotter Academy. Garcia said he'd follow on separately.

'What a cool car!' enthused Kate as she eased herself gently into the back seat. 'I'd love one of these when I'm older.'

'Me too love,' said Ken, roaring off down the drive. 'Daniel Drewsome's hired this one. He didn't want to lend it to me, but Dottie said the blacked-out windows would stop any nosy parkers peering in. We've all been to sworn to secrecy, you know. None of the other competitors have the foggiest you're here.'

Kate shivered with apprehension. It felt like forever since that day on the lake. The others might not take too kindly to her waltzing back in at the last minute. Well, she was pretty sure Sophy would be OK about it. But Astoria would be enraged.

'Are you OK, love?' asked Linda, grabbing hold of Kate's hands. 'Your hands feel like blocks of ice. Come on, what can we do to keep your mind off everything?'

'How about my new Cliff Richard CD?' suggested Ken, trying to be helpful. 'I brought it with me specially. I always think that Cliff is perfect for soothing the nerves.'

Kate and Linda both burst out laughing.

'Ken, you're a marvel,' chuckled Linda. 'You've done the trick. You've brought a smile back to our Kate's face.'

The Starspotter Academy was teeming with people.

178

Just like the Saturday before, the ballroom had been transformed into a makeshift TV studio. Cameramen, sound people, the floor manager and his team and a couple of junior producers were rushing about like headless chickens getting everything ready for nine a.m.

Astoria, Sophy, Scooter and Tommy had all been through wardrobe and make-up and now they'd assembled in the girls' dorm for a final briefing from Daniel and Dottie.

'Three instructions from me,' barked Daniel like a sergeant-major. 'One: Sing your socks off. Two: Look straight at the camera. Three: *SMILE*.'

Dottie fixed her eyes on the foursome. She was proud of them. They'd come an awfully long way in the last ten days. Without exception, they'd transformed themselves from gifted amateurs into highly-skilled professionals. But which of them was going to win?

Dottie looked at her watch. It was eight forty-five. Fifteen minutes to go before transmission.

'Right,' she said. 'I'll take you down to the ballroom and explain exactly where we want you to stand.'

Inside the ballroom, Zaza and Didi were having a quick run-through of their own. The one disadvantage of being away from London was that they couldn't use an autocue. The presenters had mini earpieces to receive updates and prompts from Daniel and Dottie, but they'd both had to learn a script for a change. This had tested Zaza to the limit. She'd spent hours going over her lines.

'What order are the kids appearing in again?' inquired Zaza as Daniel and Dottie accompanied the finalists into the ballroom.

Dottie groaned inwardly. What were the chances of Zaza getting through today's show without a hitch? Extremely remote, by her reckoning.

'Sophy, Tommy, Scooter, Astoria, K ...' shouted

179

Daniel, then stopped abruptly in his tracks.

'And Kate last?' queried Zaza.

'Don't be an idiot, Zaza,' shouted Daniel. 'You know Kate's left the show…'

Dottie winked desperately at Zaza. She'd told the presenter repeatedly that Kate's appearance was a closely-guarded secret – 'to add to the creative tension,' as Daniel put it.

At last the mists cleared and Zaza got the message.

'Oh yeah,' she said, winking back. 'Silly me. I forgot.'

Zaza and Didi had both pulled out all the stops with their outfits today. Didi, who'd twisted both Sue and Charlotte's arms to get first choice, was wearing a skin-tight black leather cat suit, trimmed with feathers. And Zaza wasn't far behind in a white mini-skirt with a leopard-skin crop top and matching over-the-knee boots.

'Right, ten seconds to go,' called Bryan, the floor manager. 'Ten, nine, eight …'

Watching from the sidelines, Dottie adjusted her headphones and then whispered good luck to Scooter, Tommy, Astoria and Sophy.

'I'll be rooting for you all. Give it everything you've got.'

'Hiya everybody,' screeched Zaza, as the credits faded from the screen and Daniel Drewsome gave her the signal to begin. 'Hiya from the Lake District. The sun is shining, the birds are singing and have we got a fantastic show lined up for you.'

'That's right,' yelled Didi, pitching her voice even louder than Zaza's. 'The big day's arrived at last … and it's going to be absolutely mega.'

'Sure is,' agreed Zaza. 'So let's get down to business. There's no time to lose. We're going to kick off with a little interview with our fab contestants – and then, one by one, they're going to sing for you.'

'Yeah,' said Didi, fiddling with one of her hoop earrings. 'And later on, once you've heard them all, we're going to open the phone lines. You can text or phone to vote for your favourite. *MAKE SURE YOU VOTE*!'

Zaza teetered across to the side of the ballroom, trying desperately not to let on how uncomfortable her leopard-skin boots were. She really ought to have spent a bit more time getting used to them. They were agony.

'Now, the first contestant we're going to talk to is the lovely Sophy McBride. You'll remember that she's fourteen and lives on the island of Colonsay in the Hebrides.'

Sophy stepped briskly forward to the microphone. She looked gorgeous in a pale pink minidress that showed off her figure to perfection.

'So what's been the best bit of Starspotter, Sophy?' asked Zaza.

'The singing lessons with Garcia Andrew,' replied Sophy. 'He's such a good teacher. Really patient and kind. And so inspiring. I've learned loads.'

'Wicked,' grinned Zaza. 'And the worst bit?'

In Sophy's mind there was no question about the worst bit of the past ten days. Her skin went icy-cold at the memory of Kate plunging into the water. She'd never forget it. But Daniel had ordered that on no account must they mention Kate's accident on air so she quickly racked her brains for something else to say.

'That's easy,' she retorted. 'Scooter's jokes. They're the corniest in the universe. Unbearable in fact.'

After Sophy, it was Tommy's turn to be interviewed by Didi. The handsome blond teenager had come on leaps and bounds during the course of the show and now charmed everyone with his simple heartfelt tribute to his mum and dad.

'I couldn't have done any of this without their support,'

he told Didi. 'Especially my mum. It was her that encouraged me to enter. Well, forced more like.'

Astoria glowered at this remark. How dare Tommy
steal her line? What was she going to say now?

Next up was Scooter, looking surprisingly smart in an
electric blue teddy boy suit. When he sidled up to chat to
Zaza, she asked him for his best joke.

'Sophy says your jokes are the worst in the universe. So
maybe you'd better let the audience at home be the judge.
But keep it clean, won't you?'

Scooter grinned indignantly.

'Hey, what d'you take me for? And what do you call
someone who keeps a dictionary in their knickers?'

Zaza looked blank, which admittedly wasn't unusual.

'Haven't a clue.'

'Smarty Pants!'

At home in South London, Giselle and Denis Lennox were
on the edges of their seats, impatient for their daughter to
appear onscreen. They'd moved the telly out of Astoria's
bedroom while she was away and into the sitting room.

Denis reckoned he knew exactly how Astoria must be
feeling right now. He'd spent enough years as a TV
warm-up guy to appreciate what she was going through.
If anything, he reflected, the longer he spent in showbiz
the more frayed his nerves became. How would Astoria
cope with the strain?

The Lennoxes hadn't heard a word from Astoria for the
past ten days – not so much as a postcard. Giselle dashed
to pick up the post the moment it landed on the mat every
morning but there had been nothing. Not a dickybird.

'No news is good news,' Denis kept saying, but it didn't
help.

'I'll be so relieved when she's home,' fretted Giselle.
She'd been trying to concentrate on what the other

finalists were saying but so far everything had gone in one ear and out of the other.

Denis leaned further forward.

'Ssssh. I think it's her turn now.'

Giselle clutched hold of Denis's hand.

'I can't bear to watch,' she muttered. 'It's too much.'

Finally Astoria appeared on the screen. With her head held high and her back as straight as a ballet dancer's, Giselle and Denis watched her breeze across to join Didi as if she hadn't a care in the world.

'Oh my goodness,' gasped Giselle. 'Asti looks so beautiful. Her hair looks like …'

Giselle stopped in mid-sentence as she gazed at Astoria's long flowing hair. No words seemed adequate to describe her glittering daughter.

'… Like spun silk,' said Denis. 'She's a star in the making, that girl of ours. No doubt about it.'

'That's an amazing outfit, Astoria,' said Didi, beaming at her protégé.

Astoria glanced down at her sparkly hot-pants and matching halter-neck top.

'Thanks Didi,' she said modestly. 'The wardrobe girls at *Rise and Shine* have really done me proud today. I'd like to say a big thank you to them.'

Standing out of view of the cameras, Scooter grimaced.

'Yuk,' he whispered to Sophy. 'I'm going to be sick. Sue and Charlotte told me Astoria had a right old tantrum this morning. Just because they'd given her the wrong colour tights. Talk about playing up to the camera.'

Meanwhile Didi was asking Astoria who had been her greatest influence. A wave of panic swept over Astoria. Tommy had already paid tribute to his mum and dad. She couldn't say the same thing. A split second later, however, inspiration struck.

'You, Didi,' gushed Astoria. 'If I can only be half as successful and lovely as you, then I'll be happy.'

Scooter scowled even more at Astoria's sickening toadying.

'That girl,' he groaned. 'If she wins, I'll … I'll … Oh I don't know what I'll do.'

As Didi drew the chat with Astoria to a close, it was Zaza's turn once more.

'Now we've got to the really exciting part,' she said. 'It's time for our wonderful Starspotter gang to show what they can really do. So let's give it up for Sophy McBride.'

The air of tension in the ballroom was palpable as Sophy took centre-stage. Dottie nodded approvingly at her. Daniel had been absolutely right to make Sophy go first. She was the eldest of the group by several months and it showed in her steady, mature attitude. Over the past few days she'd rehearsed her routine until it was spot on – there were no worries there.

Sophy had chosen to sing the tricky Atomic Kitten hit *Whole Again*. As the lights dimmed, the ballroom was magically transformed into a mini-disco, with glitter balls flashing and illuminated stars forming a spectacular backdrop. Considering how nervous she'd felt earlier, Sophy put on a sensational show. She might not win, thought Dottie as the canned applause died away, but she definitely had a chance of making it in the competitive world of showbiz. There was no doubt about it.

Tommy's performance wasn't so polished. His dance routine was as impressive as ever, culminating in an amazing backward somersault, but he hit a couple of dodgy notes in the middle. He knew as much – he gave Dottie a gloomy thumbs-down sign when he walked off. As for Scooter, he came on and gave a typically Scooterish rendition of the old Dexy Midnight Runners' number *Come On Eileen*, complete with a bit of pogo dancing halfway through.

And then it was Astoria's turn.

True to form, she looked utterly relaxed as the camera zoomed in on her. Ten days at the Academy hadn't made Dottie like Astoria any more than she had to start with. But there was no doubting the youngster's star quality. It had been apparent at the auditions and it was even more evident now. She had everything – the looks, the talent *and* the drive.

Astoria's choice of song was characteristically ambitious. She'd gone for Kylie Minogue's disco number *Can't Get You Out Of My Head*. Garcia had tried to steer her away from it in favour of something less demanding but Astoria wouldn't have it.

Watching her barnstorming performance, even Garcia was forced to concede that Astoria had been right to stick to her guns. Every single note was bang in tune and she had just the right kind of cuteness to carry the song off. Kylie herself couldn't have done it better.

As the music faded away the camera swung across to Zaza. The presenter's grey-blue eyes shone with admiration.

'Thank you Astoria Lennox,' she yelled. 'I'm sure everyone at home will agree that was quite something. And now, we've got an extra special surprise for *Rise and Shine* fans. Make sure you stay tuned because you're going to like it.'

But Didi wasn't ready to move on. Even though it wasn't in the script, she couldn't resist adding her own tribute.

'I reckon Astoria's going to be a hard act to follow, Zaza,' she trilled. 'We could be looking at a winner there.'

From the shadows, Daniel gave Didi a frantic 'speed it up' signal. What was she playing at, giving Astoria preferential treatment like that? And they still had so much to get through. There wasn't a second to waste.

'So what's the surprise we've got in store?' said Didi, smoothly returning to the script once more.

'Well,' said Zaza. 'I'm sure the viewers at home have read an awful lot about our fifth contestant in the papers this week. Most of it nonsense, to tell you the truth.'

'Yes,' said Didi, reciting Daniel's lines carefully. 'It's perfectly true that after last week's show, our five fantastic finalists enjoyed a fun day out on Lake Valewater, just a few hundred yards from where we're standing. Let's give you a taste of what they got up to.'

Daniel Drewsome had spent a whole day poring over the film Sean and his crew had taken of the *Lady Christina* trip. He and Sean had then cut and pasted the tape back together, completely missing out the moment when Kate was swept into the lake. In Daniel's version, the youngsters chatted and laughed merrily as they were showered with water. Sophy waved at a passing dinghy and Tommy offered everyone a Polo. As for Kate, there was a split second shot of her at the bow and then the film switched to her giggling at something Scooter had said.

'So there you have it,' said Zaza. 'A great day out. Nothing untoward at all. And just to show you that Kate's on tip-top form, *HERE SHE IS* ... the lovely Kate Barnsley, singing for Starspotter ...'

The whole ballroom went deathly quiet as Kate emerged from the shadows wearing a plain lilac mini-dress and flat silver sandals that laced up her calves like a Roman centurion. The whole effect was subtle, understated – and stunning. Dottie nodded in approval. Kate's outfit made Astoria's sparkly blue hot-pants look vulgar and over the top.

Immediately Kate launched into the song that Garcia had selected for her. While the others had gone for upbeat numbers with flashy backing tracks, he'd advised her to choose something as simple as possible.

'You need something really classy,' he'd said. 'How about *Don't Speak*? You know, the Gwen Stefani one.'

It was the perfect choice. Linda wiped a tear from her eye as she watched her daughter pour her heart and soul into the haunting song about love and loss. With her silver sandals twirling in GG's dance routine and her voice more powerful than ever, Kate was simply dazzling. A star in the making.

'Thank you, Kate,' beamed Zaza after Kate had taken her bow. 'That was … what can I say? That was *amazing* …'

'And there's something we need to ask you,' said Didi. 'How are you feeling now? You got a bit of a soaking in the lake this week, didn't you?'

Kate gritted her teeth. This was the tricky bit – the bit she didn't want to talk about.

'Just a bit of fun, that's all,' she said, crossing her fingers behind her back and trying to grin. 'I don't know why the papers made such a fuss about everything. I'm absolutely fine …'

Didi would have liked to quiz Kate a little more but Zaza was having none of it.

'Right, Kate, we'd better move on. It's nine fifty-five – time we got the voting started. Look closely at your screens, everyone. Here come the numbers again to vote for your favourites.'

Nonplussed at the way Zaza was asserting her authority for a change, Didi obediently ran through the list of telephone numbers.

'And you can text too,' said Zaza. 'If you want Sophy to win, text SOPHY, if you want Tommy to win, text TOMMY, and so on …'

'You've got thirty minutes to decide,' added Didi. 'The phone lines will close at ten twenty-five and we'll be back on air at ten-thirty to give you an update. And then tune in at eleven for the big result.'

'It's so exciting,' said Zaza. 'I can't wait. Can you?'

As the credits started to roll and Zaza and Didi waved goodbye, Sophy, Tommy and Scooter couldn't wait any longer. They rushed across to Kate and bombarded her with questions.

'I'm so glad to see you,' shrieked Sophy, giving her a huge hug. 'Where have you been? There were so many rumours flying around. I was really worried about you.'

'We all were,' said Tommy. 'Are you sure you're OK? It wasn't the same without you.'

The only person who didn't utter a word in the mêlée was Astoria.

She'd really given the performance of a lifetime this morning. She'd knocked spots off everyone else. Until Kate breezed back in, that is. Which of them was going to win now?

22
Down to the Wire

DANIEL DREWSOME had hired a firm called Countline to take charge of adding up the votes. From their headquarters in London, Countline staff would receive all the calls and texts and collate the results. These would then be relayed down the line to Daniel, ready for broadcast.

Once the show was over Daniel began barking out orders left, right and centre.

'*DOTTIE*, you come with me. *I SAID NOW NOT NEXT WEEK*. Everyone else, stay in the ballroom. Yes, and that means you as well, Didi and Zaza. Don't move an inch.'

Dottie would far rather have stayed chatting companionably in the ballroom with the finalists. But when Daniel shouted 'Jump,' you didn't argue. You jumped.

'Just stay here,' she instructed the Starspotter youngsters. 'Don't wander off. And make sure you drink plenty of water. I don't want anyone getting dehydrated and weary. And just think, another hour and all this madness will be over. I bet you can't wait.'

Obeying Daniel's command, Dottie scurried down the hall and into her boss's makeshift office in the east wing. She gaped at the scene of chaos inside. In London Daniel insisted on keeping his desk minimalist and bare – he lost his temper if anyone left so much as a paperclip lying around. But this office was shambolic. Paper was littered everywhere, along with Daniel's laptop, publicity photographs of all the finalists, CDs, DVDs, throat lozenges, bottles of water, you name it.

Dottie didn't comment on the mayhem. One smart remark from her and Daniel would most likely fly off the handle. And with less than an hour to go before the winner was announced, Daniel losing his rag wouldn't help anyone. Especially not her.

'Nice office, Daniel,' she said airily.

'You what?'

Daniel was busy sifting through mounds of paper, looking for something.

'Ah, here it is,' he said, pulling out a sheet of paper with the words *Press Release* emblazoned across the top. 'Look, Dottie, can you read this? Just to check the details.'

Dottie sat down opposite Daniel and read the first line of the press release.

'Young singer Astoria Lennox today walked away with The Rise and Shine Saturday Show's prestigious Starspotter award …'

She stared at her boss, completely flummoxed.

'What on earth are you playing at, Daniel? The voting's hardly begun and you've authorised some poxy public relations outfit to write a press release saying Astoria's won. What's going on?'

Daniel regarded her as if butter wouldn't melt in his mouth.

'Don't be silly, Dottie. Nothing's going on. But surely you realise that Astoria's bound to win. Her performance this morning was head and shoulders above the rest of them.'

'What about Kate?' said Dottie, indignant on Kate's behalf. '*She* was brilliant too.'

Daniel leaned back in his chair and considered what Dottie had just said.

'Yes,' he said. 'Kate *was* brilliant too. I think Astoria has got the edge, that's all.'

'You're not going to do anything shifty, are you?' said Dottie, her voice urgent now. 'You're not going to fiddle the results so Astoria wins?'

A furious look appeared on Daniel's face.

'I can't believe you just said that, Dottie. How long have we worked together?'

'Nearly three years,' said Dottie quietly.

'Exactly – and I hope you know me well enough by now to appreciate that I would never do anything as crooked as that. I know I'm a hard boss to work for, and yes, I know I sometimes get things wrong. But I promise you this, Dottie, whoever gets the most votes today wins. It could be Astoria and it could be Kate. I don't mind. They're both hugely talented girls. I've just got a hunch that it's going to be Astoria …'

'So if Kate wins, you'll send out a press release to all the papers saying that Kate's the winner,' said Dottie.

'Of course. Look, here's another version of it.'

Daniel passed Dottie a second piece of paper headed *Press Release*.

'*Young singer Kate Barnsley today walked away with* The Rise and Shine Saturday Show*'s prestigious Starspotter award* …'

Dottie felt as if a huge weight had been lifted from her shoulders.

'I never doubted you for a second, Daniel,' she beamed, lying through her teeth.

At ten twenty-nine Daniel and Dottie dashed down the hall to give the *Rise and Shine* presenters an update on the voting so far.

'Here, Didi,' said Daniel. 'Here's your script. Read straight from the top. You give the latest voting figures and then Zaza, you tell everyone to tune in at eleven for the final result. OK?'

Didi's heart leapt as she glanced at the figures Daniel had given her. They were exactly what she'd hoped to see.

'Come on, Zaza, we're on in thirty seconds,' she yelled, grabbing hold of Zaza's hand and pulling her towards the ballroom.

Giselle Lennox was almost hyperventilating by the time Didi and Zaza appeared onscreen for the ten-thirty update. She'd dialled up countless times to vote for Astoria and now she was exhausted.

'I might have to go and lie down,' she told her husband. 'I don't think I can cope with much more of this waiting. It's too stressful.'

As Giselle got to her feet, Denis caught hold of her hand.

'You're not going anywhere, love. Just listen. This is the most important day in our daughter's life ...'

He stopped in mid-sentence as Didi began her progress report on the voting.

'Thank you so much to everyone for voting,' said Didi. 'You've voted in your hundreds of thousands, which is fantastic. We haven't got all the results at the Academy yet but it's as close as a whisker. All the contestants have had huge support. But two of them are neck and neck, ahead of the others. D'you want to know who the two front-runners are?'

'We sure do, Didi,' said Zaza happily. 'Go on. Spill the beans.'

'Out in front by a considerable margin are ...'

'Sorry,' giggled Zaza. 'We're not going to tell you. Not yet, anyway. You'll have to tune in at eleven to find out.'

Back in Daniel's office, Dottie drummed the desk with her fingers.

'Any news?'

Daniel scrolled down his computer screen for the umpteenth time.

'Yep,' he said. 'The final result's come through. I think she's done it.'

Now that the moment of truth was here, Dottie wasn't sure she wanted to know. She scrutinised Daniel's face, trying to work out the result from his expression.

'It's Astoria, isn't it?' she said finally.

'Yep. 'Fraid so.'

Dottie's shoulders slumped with disappointment. She was well aware it was unprofessional to favour Kate, but she couldn't help herself. Kate so deserved this special chance. Astoria, with her stage school background and indulgent parents, would probably make it in showbiz anyway. But Kate would probably slink off back to Gribblesdale and never be heard of again.

'What were the votes?' asked Dottie glumly.

Daniel consulted his screen again.

'It's quite incredible,' he said. 'There are only nine votes between them. Almost too close to call.'

'We'd better go and get everyone ready for the big announcement then,' said Dottie, getting up to go.

At that moment, however, the phone on Daniel's desk rang.

'Who the hell's ringing now?' he demanded.

'How do I know? I know I'm lots of things, but I'm not telepathic.'

'Daniel Drewsome,' snarled Daniel into the receiver. 'What the hell d'you want? Haven't you caused enough trouble already?'

'Who is it?' mouthed Dottie.

Daniel covered the mouthpiece with his hand.

'I can't believe the man's cheek,' he said. 'It's Scooter Mason's dad. You know, Bill Mason from the *Daily*

193

Despatch. How did he get this number? I only gave it to a handful of people.'

Dottie sat down again abruptly. Scooter had denied everything but Dottie was ninety-nine per cent sure that it was him who'd tipped his dad off about Kate's accident on the lake. What did the troublemaking hack want now?

'You've got precisely thirty seconds,' said Daniel. 'So you'd better make it quick.'

As Dottie watched Daniel's face turn more and more ashen, she tried to work out what on earth Bill Mason was up to.

'Yep,' said Daniel. 'Yep. Yep. You bet. OK. You can run the story. Yep. Your exclusive. Yep. Well, I suppose it's better that it's come out now rather than later.'

Finally, Daniel slammed down the phone so hard that it bounced off its cradle.

'Blast, blast, blast, blast, blast,' he shouted at the hapless Dottie. 'Why on earth did I ever come up with this stupid Starspotter idea? Everything's collapsing around my ears.'

'Daniel,' said Dottie firmly. 'Could you kindly tell me what the blooming heck is going on?'

Daniel sighed heavily.

'You know when we launched Starspotter back in March we made it quite clear what the rules of entry were?'

Dottie nodded.

'Of course,' she said quickly. 'None of the entrants could be professional singers or dancers already. And they weren't allowed to have had a record released or appeared on TV before. So what?'

'And did we ever check the finalists out? Check that they hadn't done any of those things?'

Now it was Dottie's turn to look stunned. She banged her head with the side of her fist. She'd been so sure they'd covered everything.

'Well, no. We just assumed that they'd follow the rules. But none of them are professional singers or dancers, are they? And I'm pretty sure that they haven't had a record released or appeared on TV before.'

'That's precisely where you're wrong, Dottie,' muttered Daniel wearily. 'Bill Mason's just told me that Astoria used to belong to a dance troupe called the Marionettes. It was five or six years ago but they had a regular slot on Bobby Ballard's chat show. The *Despatch* have unearthed a video from somewhere.'

Dottie stared disbelievingly at Daniel.

'So she *has* appeared on TV before?'

'Looks like it. Idiotic girl. It doesn't sound as if it amounted to anything much though. Shall we just turn a blind eye? Ignore it?'

Dottie was absolutely outraged.

'Rules are rules,' she told Daniel. 'If Astoria's been on TV before she isn't eligible to enter Starspotter.'

'I suppose,' said Daniel gloomily.

'So why on earth did she?'

Daniel rolled his eyes at the ceiling.

'Who knows? Maybe it slipped her mind. Maybe she thought it was so long ago it didn't count.'

'So what are we going to do?'

'Run away?' said Daniel wearily. 'That's what I feel like. Why don't the two of us run away and leave the rest of the team to sort out the mess?'

23
Tears and Tantrums

IT WAS one minute to eleven and the finalists were shaking with nerves. Kate had stopped biting her nails ages ago but she was so jumpy that she'd bitten every nail to the quick on her left hand and was about to start on her right. Scooter and Tommy were playing cards to keep their minds off the verdict. Sophy was doodling on an old newspaper she'd found and Astoria was driving everyone potty humming the chorus from *Can't Get You Out Of My Head* over and over again.

'You're doing *my* head in – shut up, will you?' Scooter shouted rudely at Astoria but she took no notice.

At that moment Dottie bustled into the ballroom and briskly told them to gather in a group alongside Didi and Zaza.

'Whatever the result, I want you all to smile as if your whole lives depended on it,' she instructed them. 'No tears and no tantrums. Do you understand? That's an order.'

The five youngsters nodded.

'Are you going to tell us who's won before Didi and Zaza announce it officially?' asked Sophy.

'Certainly not,' said Dottie.

For the final time, Bryan, the floor manager, started the countdown. 'Ten seconds to go, everyone. Ten, nine, eight, seven…'

Sophy grabbed Kate's hand and held it tight. Kate grinned at her and tried to take hold of Astoria's in turn.

196

But Astoria was having none of it and edged closer to Tommy.

'A big welcome back to everybody,' screeched Didi.

'I don't know about the viewers at home but here at the Starspotter Academy we're all on absolute tenterhooks,' said Zaza. 'Just which of these five super-talented young people has won our fab competition? Who is the lucky winner who will walk away from the academy today with an amazing new wardrobe, a holiday in the Caribbean with their family… and best of all, a record deal?'

Astoria gulped nervously. Surely it was going to be her? It *must* be her.

Didi waved a sheaf of papers at the camera.

'I've got the results right here. So without further ado let's find out who the winning Starspotter is.'

'Are you all right?' Sophy whispered to Kate. 'You're shaking.'

'Sorry,' mumbled Kate. 'I just wish they'd hurry up and get on with it.'

'Me too.'

Zaza had now turned to face the five youngsters. She had protested to Daniel that it was too cruel to prolong their agony but he'd curtly ordered her not to argue.

'Tommy,' said Zaza.

Instantly Tommy's face lit up. He'd thought his performance had been a bit second-rate. He couldn't have won, could he?

'I'm afraid it's not you,' said Zaza.

'Sophy,' said Didi.

Sophy shook her head at Kate. She'd done her best but she doubted it was good enough to win.

'It's not you.'

'And Scooter,' said Zaza. 'No, it isn't you, either.'

'So that leaves us with our final two contestants,' said Didi. 'Astoria and Kate. Will you kindly step forward?'

197

Once again, Kate tried to take Astoria's hand – just to show that they were friends and not rivals. For a split second Astoria let her, then shook Kate off again. She didn't want any soppy stuff now – not in her moment of triumph.

Zaza stared directly at the camera once more.

'We now have a very serious announcement,' she said, her face solemn for once. It is going to be hugely disappointing for one of these two girls so we have asked Daniel Drewsome, the producer of *The Rise and Shine Saturday Show* to make it.'

Kate and Astoria stared at each other uncomprehendingly. This was weird. What the blazes was going on?

They watched Daniel Drewsome stride on to the set. Wearing his trademark black T-shirt and black leather trousers, he looked more scary than ever.

Daniel stared at Kate and Astoria for a couple of seconds before speaking.

'It is my very great pleasure to announce the winner of our wonderful Starspotter competition. I am very pleased indeed that this contest has given a group of exceptionally talented youngsters the chance to be coached by some of the best voice and dance teachers in the business. I'm certain too, that whichever one of these two brilliant girls wins, they will both go on to have stupendous showbiz careers.'

Standing in the wings, Linda Barnsley sobbed quietly. She'd never felt so proud.

'I'm afraid, however, that only one of them can win. It is going to be very disappointing for the loser – especially when we explain our reasons – but here at *Rise and Shine* we pride ourselves on sticking to our word. And that's what we intend to do.

'When the votes were counted – hundreds of thousands of them – there were only nine votes separating Astoria

Lennox and Kate Barnsley. And it was Astoria who came out on top …'

Astoria's face was instantly wreathed in a huge smile. She stepped forward in triumph with her hands with held aloft. She'd done it.

But Daniel wagged his finger at her to stop.

'I'm sorry,' he said. 'Not so fast, Astoria. I'm sad to say that this isn't the end of the story. When we launched Starspotter nearly six months ago, we stipulated that certain people were barred from entering.'

A panic-stricken look suddenly appeared in Astoria's eyes. This didn't sound promising.

'We said entrants couldn't be professional singers or dancers already. And we insisted they couldn't have had a record released or performed on TV before.'

Astoria opened her mouth to speak then shut it again quickly as Daniel continued speaking.

'It's come to our notice in the last fifteen minutes that Astoria used to be a member of a dance group called the Marionettes. She was only six at the time but on a number of occasions the Marionettes appeared on a TV chat show. I'm sorry, Astoria, but we have to stick by the rules. I'm afraid you don't fulfil the entry requirements to take part in Starspotter …'

At this point Astoria burst into floods of tears.

'But it's not fair,' she wailed. 'I can hardly remember the Marionettes. I was only six. It doesn't count …'

Daniel glanced at Astoria anxiously. He wasn't convinced that a twelve-year-old weeping because she'd lost the Starspotter title made good TV. And he certainly didn't want the television watchdogs making a complaint.

'What we are saying is that Astoria Lennox will be a superstar in the future – we're certain of that. But the winner of *Rise and Shine*'s Starspotter competition, and a very worthy winner too, is … *KATE BARNSLEY*.'

At Daniel's words, the entire ballroom erupted. All the other finalists – apart from Astoria, who was still sobbing – scooped Kate up in their arms and hoisted her on to Tommy's shoulders. A panoply of glittery silver stars descended from the ceiling, like a spectacular rainstorm, and Dottie began chanting. 'Three cheers for Kate. Hip hip hooray…'

Hovering in the background, Linda couldn't bear to be parted from her daughter for a single second longer. She darted across the set screaming 'Kate, you did it … you did it …'

Kate gestured frantically to Tommy to let her down. And then, when her feet were on firm ground once more, she raced straight into her mum's arms. The two of them stood clutching each other, oblivious to the Starspotter gang, oblivious to Dottie and the rest of the crew, oblivious to the world.